LUNAR BRACEROS
2125 – 2148

ROSAURA SÁNCHEZ
AND
BEATRICE PITA

ILLUSTRATIONS BY MARIO A. CHACON

All rights reserved. No part of this publication may be stored in a retrieval system, transmitted or reproduced in any way, including but not limited to photocopy, photograph, magnetic, laser or other type of record, without prior agreement and written permission of the publisher.

Floricanto is a trademark of Floricanto Press. Berkeley Press is an imprint of Inter-American Development, Inc.

Floricanto Press

7177 Walnut Canyon Rd

Moorpark, California 93021

(415) 793-2662

www.FloricantoPress.com

"Por nuestra cultura hablarán nuestros libros. Our books shall speak for our culture." Roberto Cabello-Argandoña and Leyla Namazie, Editors

Design and layout by Cal A. Vera.
Photo of cover art by Manuel "Memo" Cavada.

To: Alex, Rubén & Nelda
To: Joseph, Aaron & Andrew

"Space by itself, and time by itself, are doomed to fade away into mere shadows, and only a kind union of the two will preserve an independent reality."

- Albert Einstein

June 2148

Tío, my mother left me these nanotexts with lunar posts, lessons, bits and pieces of conversations, and notations with friends who sent them to me after she and my Dad went up North eight years ago. I put them all together and I've been reading them over and over, and now I think it's time you read them. I hope these will reach you through our clandestine network. I hope to see you soon.

THERE WERE SEVEN OF US. Our particular lunar transport landed late in 2125. We were the fourth crew of lunar braceros sent to the Moon to work on the waste and toxic landfills sent up from Earth. Sometimes we called ourselves the Tecos or the "techs," and sometimes, for good reason, "the motley crew" – you'll see why. Down here on Earth they'd long since exceeded the capacity to store waste products, so when they couldn't find any more places in Periphery to warehouse the stuff, plans were made to ship it to the Moon. The plan was to develop sublunar deposit sites, similar to the ones they had carved out in the Arizona and Sonoran deserts. At the beginning of the project, back in 2112, they tried carving out the sites with remote detonators from lunar orbit; once the holes were created, they planned on using robotic bulldozers and earthmovers to shovel out the lunar soil or sand. In these excavated areas, robotic units were supposed to assemble prefabricated subterranean — or rather, sublunar — containment compounds, with com centers, walkways, and bunkers that would house several containers and specialized tanks for each type of waste: carcinogens, radioactives and what had been deemed non-recyclables, but the plans didn't really work out. The biggest problem from way back at the program's inception, and to date, wasn't just finding sites for the waste, but getting it to the Moon. Logistics. The excavations needed to be pretty precisely done; the engineers and planners out in orbit could not depend on the robotic units that kept breaking down. What were needed were hands-on workers who could adapt to changing lunar situations and were capable of solving unforeseen problems. That's where we came in. We could trouble-shoot, and we were cheaper.

Lunar colonization really geared up after what back then was called "The Great Political Restructuring" — I always loved the slogans they came up with — that began with the creation of the new nation-state of "Cali-Texas," the formation of a new political entity that included several of the northern Mexican states (Tamaulipas, Coahuila, Chihuahua, Nuevo Leon, Sonora and Baja California), and the former U.S. Southwest states: Texas, Colorado, New Mexico, Arizona, was behind the new political re-alignment; the push, and the hype that went along with it, came from the transnational agri-business corporations and the four big bio-techs, companies that controlled anything and everything that had to do with technology transfer, informatics and any kind of power generation, bio-fuel, nuclear or otherwise. Utah, California, Nevada, as well as Oregon, Washington, Alaska and Hawaii. Everybody knew who was behind the new political re-alignment; the push, and the hype that went along with it, came from the transnational agri-business corporations and the four big bio-techs, companies that controlled anything and everything that had to do with technology transfer, informatics and any kind of power generation, bio-fuel, nuclear or otherwise.

))))))))))))

YES, CALI-TEXAS. THAT'S WHERE WE'RE FROM, FRANK AND I, LETICIA AND MAGGIE, BETTY AND TOM, JED, SAM, AND JAKE. SOMEDAY YOU'LL GO THERE TO LIVE WITH YOUR UNCLE RICARDO AND MY PARENTS AND LUPITA. YOU'LL GO TO COLLEGE THERE AS WELL. FRANK AND I WILL BE SOMEWHERE NEAR. YOU DON'T HAVE TO WORRY ABOUT THAT. THAT'S WHAT I ALWAYS TOLD HIM.

))))))))))))

During the twenty-first century astronomers found over 700 planets in other solar systems, most many, many light-years from Earth. The goal of astronomers was to find a planet similar to ours, that is, at approximately the same distance from its sun, with a similar mass and with a habitable zone and water. Many of the planets found were much larger than Earth, some even several times as large as Jupiter and made up mostly of hydrogen and helium gas. During the twenty-first century we sent telescopes into space to monitor the constellation Cygnus as well as other instruments, like the one designed for the Space Interferometry Mission to find Earth-like planets around closer stars. Astronomers also created the Terrestrial Planet Finder, launched around the early part of the twenty-first century, to take pictures of Earth-like planets. Once such a planet was found there would be a Search for Extraterrestrial Intelligence; already in the 20th and 21st centuries, SETI had developed hundreds of radio telescopes designed to search for radio signals from an advanced civilization thousands of light years away.

The Space Laboratory on the Moon was involved in all these research projects and we sometimes had a chance to hear about the latest findings from Marcy, who was a Research Assistant at the lab. Working on her dissertation in Astro-Engineering, she hoped to be among the first to find an Earth twin, or as she called it, Plan B.

Some lab assistants were studying solar winds, spatial turbulence (the Gibson effect), and the magnetic waves that accelerate them and propel streams of electrically charged gas away from the sun. These solar storms can have lethal consequences, especially for those of us on the Moon. That's why predicting major solar events can be a matter of life and death. Other Lab assistants were working on cosmic rays bearing energies millions of times larger than any particle accelerator on Earth. Astronomers had previously determined that these active galactic nuclei, able to gobble up energy from the surrounding space and spit it out with tremendous force, were coming from a type of black hole found at the center of some particular galaxies. While the

Earth's atmosphere served as a shield, preventing the particles from reaching the surface, this was not the case on the Moon. The highest-energy particles, called the OhMy-God particles, did strike Earth occasionally, but on the Moon it was possible to trace these particles as well as the course of the secondary particles that do cascade on Earth whenever a high-energy cosmic ray hits the upper atmosphere. While we could spot them visually from our station, as lowly lunar braceros we did not of course have the sophisticated instruments to track them. Some were said to come from Centaurus A, a galaxy about 13.7 million light-years away. Finding the specific sources is still an important research objective and something that maybe you, my son, will be able to work on. But for that you will need to get back to work on your algorithmic functions. No more stalling, m'hijo.

⋅ ⋅ ⟩ ⟩ ⟩ ⟩ ▶ ▶ ● ● ● ● ●

Okay, back to your history lesson. I suppose I don't have to tell you when and how all of this came down, but I'll repeat myself, in case you weren't paying attention. In part, at least, it was the result of the military coup d'etat in the U.S. in 2068, when a sector of the armed forces rose up against a U.S. Congress that had finally figured out that the New Imperial Order was undermining national interests. The NIO — made up of the ten dominant multinational consortia — had interests on a grander scale, as became all too evident when they basically took over most of Africa in 2065, making the whole of the continent, including the Saudi peninsula, its "protectorate." Expansion in Asia had been held back by the Chinese advance that had partnered up with the Russians and moved into the Southeast Asian region, without much trouble really, and was gaining control of the Indian subcontinent pretty much —despite continued Muslim uprisings in what had been Bangladesh, Afghanistan, and Pakistan.

By 2100 the Chinese had also claimed the "dark side of the Moon," had established a lunar colony and installed their own dump sites, but that's another story. Actually, our contact with the Chinese on the Moon turned out to be what enabled our return, but we'll get to that later.

— All right, Pedro, you better get some sleep. I'll pick up where we left off tomorrow, son.

— But, I'm not sleepy yet. And besides, you promised to tell me all about it before my birthday.

— That's right. You'll be 10 soon. It's almost incredible. All right, I'll tell you just a bit more.

〉〉〉〉〉〉●●●●●●

FRANK GAGGED WHEN HE OPENED THE CONTAINER AND SINCE I COULD HEAR EVERYTHING HE UTTERED, I MADE A HAND GESTURE TO ASK WHAT WAS UP AND WHEN HE DIDN'T REACT, I GRABBED HIM BY THE ARM AND PUSHED HIM ASIDE, BUT ONLY AFTER MAKING SURE OUR VIEWERS AND TRANSMITTING COM SYSTEMS WERE STILL DISCONNECTED. I THEN TOOK A LOOK FOR MYSELF. I FROZE FOR A FEW SECONDS, SHOCKED AT THE SIGHT OF THE MASS OF CORPSES IN THE CONTAINER. I KNEW I HAD TO CLOSE THE LID BEFORE THE COM SYSTEM CAME BACK ON. I SLAMMED THE TOP DOWN AND STRUGGLED TO GET TO THE DOOR WITH FRANK RIGHT BEHIND ME. I HAD TO FIGHT THE IMPULSE TO VOMIT AS IT IS DEADLY IN A SPACE SUIT. ONCE OUTSIDE WE LEANED AGAINST THE WALL OF THE BUNKER, AS OUR COM SYSTEMS CAME BACK ON. THE SHOCK OF IT HAD PARALYZED FRANK AND WE JUST STOOD THERE FOR A WHILE, TILL A VOICE CAME ON SAYING: "I TELL YOU, I LEAVE THE COM CENTER FOR A SECOND AND YOU TWO COME DOWN WITH SPACE STASIS. IS EVERYTHING ALL RIGHT?

Anyhow, by 2068, back in the good old U.S. of A., as the old timers used to say, the economy had declined to the point that the only thing the country had going for it was its military power. The NIO was pretty much calling the shots and concerned with production outside the U.S. At that point and in view of its failing economy, Congress decided to deal with the situation by reassessing its policies and closing down a number of U.S. military bases around the world; it also set out to reduce the military budget, making it difficult for the U.S. to continue its invasions for the NIO throughout the Middle East and Africa and later in Latin America. That's when the Secretary of Defense and the military's Supreme Commander

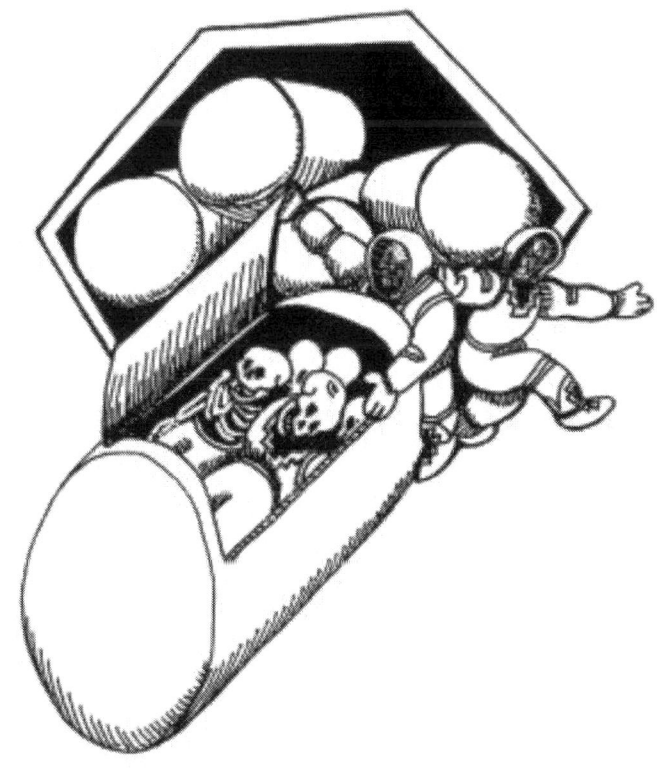

initiated a break with Congress and, with support from most of the East Coast military bases, carried out the replacement of civilian government with a military regime linked, of course, to the NIO. They were well on their way to having a powerful police state allied to global capital enterprises.

But capital often takes surprising turns. Paradoxically, it prefers a façade of democracy and consent, but that's another matter. We'll have to talk about that again at some other time. Anyhow, what happened came as a total surprise to the West coast establishment. The West Coast military, which at first seemed to go along with the coup, suddenly took another turn, perhaps, if you ask me, because most of the high tech and multinationals were based in the West and by that time highly invested with Chinese capital. The military installations in the West began questioning the new military government's orders. Can you believe it? Things got really twisted when regional Pacific Rim interests allied with segments of NIO interests kicked in, creating competition not between different national capitals, as had occurred in other centuries, but internally, between regional capitals, all ironically allied to global corporations. This competition gave rise to an all out call for secession of the West. That's when a "civil war" of sorts broke out, but of course this time it wasn't North versus South but East versus West. The "war" did not lead to all-out military conflict, which would have obliterated the entire continent, but to division, as the Western fringe of the NIO, in alliance with the Ruso-Chinese Confederation, established what came to be known as the Pacific Rim Allies Treaty (PRAT). That was also the beginning of what came to be called Cali-Texas, with the creation of a new nation-state in 2070, that soon drew in the northern Mexican states as well. That was the end of the United States as it had been known till then and within a space of 30 years, CaliTexas had become the hegemonic economy of the world, more powerful even than its ally, the Ruso-Chinese Confederation, or even the European Community, although economically (and that meant politically, as the 19th century Cuban Martí noted) it was still the re-shuffled NIO that really called the shots. All that may sound like ancient history to you, but you have to remember that it all broke apart only some thirty years before I was born.

— Now you better go to bed; you need to get some sleep, Pedro. Birthday month or not, you and Guamancito have to help weed the garden tomorrow. We're all lucky to be working on these communal lands, Pedrín. I'll tell you next time about the Reservation where I grew up. I'm turning off the light and the uplink as well. We'll continue the story another time.

))))))▶▶●●●●●

When we were kids, Space was, for us, the unknown, the universe, full of stars and planets and comets, an infinite area of exploration that would undoubtedly bring us into contact with beings of higher intelligence, more highly evolved, that would revolutionize our world and change social relations and put an end not only to our ignorance about so many things, but also, and especially, to the Reservations. Many a night we sat on our FresRes balcony, when all the lights on the Reservation were out, except in the distant outskirts, looking for UFOs, talking about life on other planets, and hoping to make contact, hopefully before we died. Simply to know what was out there would be really something, but being part of space exploration was our dream. Astrophysics was the way, but for that you needed a background in math and engineering, as well as physics. So that is what Ricardo and I planned to study. We were both good at math and science, "Surprisingly for reslifers" we were told at the time.

＞＞＞＞＞▶▶▶●●●●●

The splitting-off of half its territory led to the definitive weakening of the U.S. Not even the return of civilian government was able to lead to any meaningful recovery. Attempts were made to bring Cali-Texas back into the fold, but they all failed, and after a few years, the U.S., Canada and Mexico had no other option but to become part of the Cali-Texas commonwealth, autonomous regions but economically linked to and dependent on the hegemonic power. While those old nation states, as well as the rest of Latin America, remained supposedly politically independent, they were economically tied to Cali-Texas to an extent previously unseen. And Cali-Texas, let's not forget, was allied with China. The rapid spread of a variety of high-tech industries, on the one hand, and mining, oil and natural gas industries, on the other, throughout every Latin American nation led to greater contamination of the soil, the water and the air. Ecologically, as you know, the planet is one enormous hazmat zone. Even our little oasis here in Chinganaza cannot last too long since the Amazon and all its tributaries are now also contaminated, and transnational corporations continue to eye the remaining protected gas and oil reserves in this small area of the Amazon region.

Energy-wise the situation also became critical. The oil wells of the Caribbean, Mexico, Venezuela, Colombia, and Brazil rapidly became depleted, as did the Mid East sources and energy needs became increasingly dependent on nuclear power. The number of nuclear power stations also added to the production of radioactive waste. Soon the entire Andean region was filled to capacity with radioactive dumps, as well as the desert areas of Cali-Texas. The booming bio-fuel industry ended up making deserts of what had been breadbasket areas of much of the American continent north and south. The Amazon jungle was slowly disappearing except for some spots in eastern Ecuador and Peru and a few places in northwestern Brazil, places like this one. That's when things began changing in South America, but I'll get to that later. Wait up. Be patient. I know you want to hear about the Reservations, but I need to set out the historical context so that you can understand when they were set up. Let's take a break and get some lunch. Afterwards we need to go help out with the laundry. It's our turn, remember?

))))))▶▶●●●●●

Yes, I'll have to tell him about the reservations. They're the reason we have to go back. The Reservations were and are a type of population control camp mechanism. They were started to keep the homeless and the unemployed off the streets and off welfare. In the Reservation we were required to work at assigned tasks; some had jobs in nuclear weapon industries, chemical labs, and more routine industries. The skill-less were made to maintain the streets. Unemployed teachers were required to teach in the Reservation schools. Unemployed nurses and doctors were required to work in the Reservation clinics. The reservations are really a type of prison, surrounded by a razor wire fence that could easily be cut or even jumped. But rarely does anyone try. We knew as kids that beyond a clearing there were patrols and that if you were caught trying to run away you could be killed on the spot. Only transceiver equipped trucks and vans, with the Reservation Logo on the doors, were allowed in and out. There was also a Reservation bus, for taking out or bringing in larger groups. It was on one of those Reservation buses that Ricardo and I left the Reservation, he to start college and I to finish high school.

WE WERE SCHOLARSHIP KIDS BECAUSE OF OUR TALENTS IN MATH AND SCIENCE AT A MOMENT WHEN THESE SKILLS WERE CONSIDERED IMPORTANT TO THE STATE. IF IT HADN'T BEEN FOR OUR INTEREST IN THOSE AREAS, WE WOULD STILL BE BACK IN FRESNO. I WOULD PROBABLY BE TEACHING IN A RESERVATION HIGH SCHOOL AND RICARDO, WHO KNOWS? PERHAPS HE WOULD HAVE BEEN ABLE TO LEAVE IF HE HAD GOTTEN A JOB WITH A HIGH TECH COMPANY. ONE THING FOR SURE, HE WOULD HAVE HAD TO EARN A LOT TO EVEN THINK ABOUT GETTING US ALL OUT OF THERE.

〉〉〉〉〉▸▸▸●●●●●

Yesterday, or was it last week, whenever it was, I was telling you about the creation of Cali-Texas, right? But you wanted to hear a bit more about the Reservations. Look, I can sum it up by telling you that those of us on the streets or living in megaslums were considered expendable, a surplus population, and instead of transferring us all to a Moon colony — impossible at the time or even now — the state created internal colonial sites, the Reservations. We became a controlled laboratory labor force, like lab rats, a disciplinary society that was useful to the state; we produced not only the usual goods that had formerly been shipped South to sweatshops and assembly plants, but also high tech items not then under production elsewhere — like weapons, secret surveillance instrumentation, robotic instruments, and new telecommunication systems. Since our wages were mere subsistence wages, we were even cheaper than any labor force in Asia or Africa. Plus we were guaranteed consumers. We served many needs. Bio-labs seeking to create artificial organs, new medications, enhanced bodies, and to artificially develop new species had free reign in the Reservations. We residents could work in the production as well as serve as guinea pigs for these various R & D projects.

As I was telling you, the new Pacific Rim agreements with the Chinese ensured that no new global war was imminent; the same, however, could not be said at the regional level. As the population of the planet continued to increase, so did the number of local conflicts that decimated hundreds of thousands of people in Africa, Asia and the Middle East. Of course these local conflicts in fact served the global interests of the NIO, as they provided justification for invasions, and additional military spending, and promoted further displacements that produced millions for the reserve labor pools. As technological advances increased in the northern hemispheres, so did the need for cheap workers in the south where millions labored in assembly plants and agricultural enterprises. In what had previously been called the First World, labor needs were met by workers on the Reservations.

  The Reservations, both domestic in the Cali-Texas Confederation and in Europe, were first created around 2090 and had become fully functional by 2100 as sites for the housing of the unemployed and homeless that had been essentially squatting by taking over streets in several sectors of metropolitan areas, especially commercial sectors, and in the slums. The number of people in these Reservations grew tremendously, year by year, not because of any spike in the birthrate but because of massive unemployment and world-wide migrations. These new "vagrants" or "migros," as they were called back then, were forced into the Reservations, located throughout the Southwest, where they became, like I said, a wage-less labor pool, almost like slave labor, to be used in a variety of areas as needed and determined by corporate interests managing the Reservations. The Reservation was like a prison, except that families could leave the reservations if one of the members was offered employment and housing off the Reservation. The wage-less workers worked in exchange for shelter, meals and minimal medical services. Their children could go to school and if they were promising students would be looked over for admission to technological colleges or even universities. As you know, I was born in one of those Reservations.

The squatter problem got especially bad at just about the time that waste deposits for radioactive materials became scarce and the need to corral Migros and others and herd us into controlled population sites became critical. Waste management, population management, it was all part of the same thing in the end for the state. The unemployed were warehoused on the Reservations. The environmental crisis, on the other hand, led not to a new ecological policy but to the search for new deposit zones. Europe had already taken up all available spaces in Africa — both on land and offshore — for radioactive dumps and China took over Siberia for the cold storage of its waste. Bouncing from boom to bust, accumulated capital constantly needed to find new outlets, new areas of investment, new spatial fixes, new spheres of consumption as well as production, and of course, new waste deposit sites. That's where space hook-ups came in. Space projects like LunaSphere would serve to stimulate capital investment in high tech production of lunar modules, space crafts, lunar rovers, tanks, etc. and in the process created both high end employment and of course the need for grunts, thralls, call them whatever you want, low skill contract workers, braceros like us. The Moon became one more spatial fix for global capital.

〉〉〉〉〉▶▶●●●●●

THESE BULLET TRAINS FROM GUADALAJARA TO SANTIJUANA HAVE MADE TRAVEL EASIER. BILL WILL BE WAITING FOR US IN SANTIJUANA AND THERE FRANK AND I WILL MEET UP WITH MAGGIE AND LETICIA. JED, JAKE AND SAM WILL JOIN US IN LOS ANGELES AND THERE THE SEVEN OF US, TOGETHER AGAIN LIKE ON THE MOON, WILL GO UNDERGROUND AND JOIN THE OTHER CELLS THAT ARE WORKING TO BRING DOWN THE RESERVATION SYSTEM. WE NEED FOR BILL TO STAY IN MEXICO, JUST IN CASE WE NEED HELP LATER ON. THE SONORA DESERT OUT THERE REALLY REMINDS ME OF THE MOON-SCAPE BUT AT THE SAME TIME I'M ALREADY STARTING TO MISS OUR LUSH ANDEAN COMMONS. THE WARMTH AND THE

GREENERY THERE ARE SOMETHING THAT MY EYES YEARN FOR, AND BEING WITH YOU, MY SON. TOM AND BETTY WOULD HAVE WANTED TO COME AS WELL BUT SOMEONE HAD TO STAY BEHIND. I KNOW YOU WILL BE FINE WITH THEM AND HAPPY TO HAVE GUAMÁN AT YOUR SIDE. BE SURE TO KEEP UP YOUR STUDIES. I THINK BACK ON ALL THE SCIENCE LESSONS WE DISCUSSED, ESPECIALLY OUR CONVERSATIONS ON ASTRONOMY, YOUR FAVORITE SUBJECT. BEFORE LEAVING SANTIJUANA I WILL SEND YOU A POST AND ONCE BACK HOME BILL WILL WRITE YOU IN CODE, LIKE WE AGREED, TO LET YOU KNOW WE ARRIVED AND ARE DOING FINE. BE SAFE, PEDRITO.

( )))) ▶ ▶ ● ● ● ● ●

Your biological father, Gabriel, was born on a Reservation

too, the one in Chico, up north in California. But your father Frank was born in Calexico and his family managed to stay out of a res, thanks to an uncle up in San Francisco that had a couple of restaurants where his parents went to work. Still, life was hard for him and his brother Peter, who was several years older and not interested in going to college. Without a job, Peter was in danger of being picked up, but he managed to stay out of Res life by signing up for Moon duty as a trash-technician. Trash-techs were guaranteed subsistence, clothing, everything they needed while they worked on the Moon and in the meantime, their stipend or wage was deposited in an account for them. That's what led Peter to sign up for two tours as he hoped to have enough to start his own business, perhaps a restaurant like his uncle's or a motorcycle shop to fix bikes. Your namesake was into motorcycles, yes, much like you are into your bicycle, at least now. Who knows, maybe when you get older you too will go wild over motorcycles. I certainly hope not. Frank says your uncle almost got himself killed once when he tried to outrun a train. Yes, yes, Peter is dead, but it wasn't in that way. I know it's confusing.

OF COURSE THE BODIES THAT HAD BEEN PILED UP IN THE CONTAINER HAD RUPTURED, BUT THE SKELETONS, WITH BITS OF THEIR CLOTHING STUCK TO THE BONES, STILL CLEARLY INDICATED WHO THE MEN WERE. EACH PERSON HAD WORN A TYPE OF JUMPSUIT WITH A NAME LABEL ON THE LEFT BREAST POCKET AND THOSE, ALTHOUGH STAINED, WERE STILL VISIBLE. THE SKELETON ON TOP WITH A HOLE IN THE RIGHT LOBE HAD THE NAME PETER HO ON THE LEFT POCKET. IF THAT WAS PETER, THEN THE OTHERS WERE HIS TEAMMATES.

Come on, it's time to go do our chores in the garden. Today, remember, we're joining the weeding brigade. There's Guamancito, already set to go with his small hoe. We're clearing this new area. Remind me to tell you about our commons later tonight when we have dinner. Yes, you're right, this entire region was once conquered by the Incas way back before the Spanish colonizers arrived. Buenos días, Erlinda. Two more strong little arms for you. All right, Pedro, she'll take you over to the greenhouses while I work on the cebolla.

○))))) ▶ ▶ ● ● ● ● ●

Hey, little bro, yo mama, Lydia, sure likes complicating things, way too technical if you ask me. Up in South Sacra we had it all figured out, nice and simple. Let me tell you what really happened. Turns out the world was fully fucked and things got even worse when the military types decided to take us down the po- lice state road. But, like in all power trips, they themselves done split up into two camps, with the West fuckers having more leverage with the NIOS, you know, the rulers of the world. What could have been the end of the planet with all the parque that they both had became instead the end of us, as the new po-lice state, calling itself, Cali-Texas, began rounding us up if we didn't have a job or if we were on the street, or if we didn't earn enough, or if they needed more workers in certain industries or in certain parts of the world. So, we started living in prison labor camps, called Reservations. Reslifers they called us. But they gave some of us a choice. We could either be fucked up on Earth or fucked up on the Moon, and by that time, it didn't matter much. Same shit, different place. My compa, Sam, always one step ahead of the man, thought we'd do better on the Moon and so we signed up as heavy machine operators, although on the moon, they weren't as heavy. Oh, yeah, right, you've never been there. Keep it that way, kid. "Va 'tar chévere, Jake," he would say in his Caribbean Mexican Spanish. Y este negro se lo creyó, since Sam was the one with some schooling and a pilot's license. But, man, we almost ate it up there. Fortunately, the dude could really fly; otherwise we'd still be floating around on the Moon, or looking like peanut butter on the inside of some can by now.

⁌ ⁌ ⁌ ⁌ ⁌ ⁌ ⁌ ⁌ ⁌ ⁌ ⁌ ⁌

— Why, I'll tell you why. The Incas in pre-Columbian times divided the land into three parts, one part for the temple and priests, one part for the Inca and his family, and the rest of the land for the people. The latter was divided in equal shares. Each man received enough land for himself and upon marriage was assigned land for the couple. For every child born into the family the man received an additional portion of land. The division of land was renewed every year and portions were increased or diminished according to the numbers in the family. No, I don't really know if the women also received their portion, but it is highly likely as the portions were allotted according to the number of members, male and female. What was a yearly distribution in fact was property held throughout the lifetime of an individual. Once that person married, a new family allotment was made and so on. The people were not allowed to add to their land on their own nor to give part of it up of their own accord.

Strictly speaking, the Commons in Chinganaza does not follow the Incan model. All the land here is held in common and all those dwelling here contribute to the subsistence and maintenance of the commons in some way. All of us have duties and each one of us, both men and women, has to spend part of the day working in the fields. There is always much to do, either weeding, watering, and hoeing the fields and gardens, dividing and replanting the seedlings, trimming the trees, ridding the ground of pests, grasshoppers especially, and harvesting, all tasks you too are learning. When you are sixteen you will be asked to participate like an adult. Like their ancestors, the Quechuas of Chinganaza developed irrigation canals and subterranean aqueducts to water the crops long before we arrived. This is a valley but we are surrounded by the Cordillera and there we do what the Indians have done for centuries: terrace the hillsides for planting corn, that's choclo or maíz, as we say in Cali-Texas, the most important crop in all of the Americas, even today.

Gardening, as you know, isn't the only task assigned by our commons committee. Some of us have other duties as well, like teaching or working in the nursery or helping with the arts and crafts that are then taken by one of our agents and sold in the market place of nearby towns. Our surplus fruit is also taken to be sold but grain and other goods are kept in mountain caves that are much like cellars and keep the provisions fresh. What we get for the crafts and other surplus is used to buy cloth, shoes, medicines and sugar. As you know, we grow our own coffee and that is a lifesaver. Frank and I couldn't live without our five or six cups of coffee a day. We also grow our own tobacco and coca leaves, which we use for tea and for medicine. Some of the money received for goods pays for the electricity we get from the nearest town and it has also been used to acquire computers, like yours, and for the satellite receivers.

— You're right. Life here isn't just work. If I were to ask you, Pedro, what you like best about living here, what would you say?

— Playing soccer and baseball with my friends.

— Yeah, that's always fun, but there's also the river where we go swimming. And now, most of you kids have computers and can uplink to all kinds of programs. Show your Dad the images you found of the Moon.

— You know, Frank, our being here has undoubtedly brought changes to the commons but I think overall we're the ones who have benefited the most and been affected the most by our Quechua friends, their notion of equality and tolerance for difference. And, most of all, in this day and age, their willingness to take us in and become part of their community is really incredible. If it hadn't been for them, well, I don't know.

— What we have in Chinganaza, Pedro, was won over many years. It all began at the end of the 20th century when Indians in South America, especially in Ecuador, and in the Cantón of Guamote, rose up to demand their lands, their linguistic and cultural rights, and their political rights. The Pachakutik-New Land Movement for Multinational Unity began making gains in a variety of municipalities that became indigenous-run municipalities. What began in Guamote spread throughout Ecuador and led to the establishment of the Confederation of Indigenous Nationalities of Ecuador (CONAIE), which represented indigenous issues before the state and addressed indigenous needs and grievances. The indigenous mobilization and uprisings led to political changes way back in 2000 and to what is now a broad network of indigenous organizations. It was the growth of the indigenous movement throughout the 21st century that allowed the Amazonian populations to limit the incursions planned by transnational mining, oil and natural gas enterprises and kept them from destroying all the biodiversity of the area and from displacing thousands of indigenous villagers. This movement is what enabled the general autonomy of Chinganaza and its maintaining certain traditions and the Chinganaza commons, while other indigenous cantones took the road of so-called modernization. Economic equity has been achieved within this commons although not yet in other Amazonian sites. Nevertheless, these political changes have — believe it or not — enabled Chinganaza to survive, although there are interests that would love to take over this crucial area which is linked to Macas.

— No, I'm not idealizing the place, Frank. Get off your cynical horse. I fully recognize that we have problems here as well. The distribution of food, clothing and tools goes well, though; you have to admit. Betty has helped to make sure that all the young kids are vaccinated, but remember that time, when the fruit brokers returned with a new variant of the flu? That bug almost killed several children. You too, Pedro, were sick for many days, remember?

— No, we won't always live here, Pedro. You, for example, will leave the commons when you're eighteen. You'll be joining my brother Ricardo in Cali-Texas. He'll make sure that you get your education and that you become the astronomer that you dream of being. And then, some day perhaps you too will travel to the Moon and even beyond. Who knows? Of course, Frank and I will also be there with you, but if, for any reason, we should not be around, remember that your tío Ricardo will look after you, and make sure that you have a chance to meet your grandparents. Yes, yes, Ricardo knows all about the plan, don't worry.

〉〉〉〉〉▶▶▶●●●●

— Vem. Preciso falar com você sem que êles saibam. Você sabe que eu trabalho no nôvo laboratório, não? That's how it all started, with him talking to me in Portuguese 'cause he knew the gringo fresinhas could not speak the language much. When we were finally able to talk, he told me that the project that I had signed onto was not really interested in the development of synthetic organ tissue but in the harvesting of human organs from the villagers. He was about to present some kind of acceptable excuse to leave the project and before going he wanted me to know what was really going on. I began checking things out and found out that he was right, that what he said was what was actually happening. They were in fact setting up an organ farm. After that, I made contact with João, a social worker from Brasilia working in the village, who spoke both Portuguese and Guaraní. He would have to find a way to warn the villagers that the lab was after their organs because their antibody production was still uncompromised from exposure to antibiotics and pollution. He had to tell them that their organs would be marketed and that the younger pre-adolescent children were especially at risk. We

COMMUNICATED IN A SORT OF PORTUÑOL—SPANISH AND PORTUGUESE MIX — TO THROW PEOPLE OFF, BUT IT WAS RISKY. I DIDN'T KNOW WHAT TO DO AND WASN'T SURE IF JOÃO COULD HELP SPREAD THE WORD WITHOUT GETTING HIMSELF DISAPPEARED. I DON'T KNOW IF THIS MESSAGE WILL REACH YOU, LYDIA, BUT I'M SENDING IT IN A DIGITAL CHIP WITH AN ASSISTANT THAT WILL BE TRAVELING OUTSIDE THE VILLAGE TO BRING BACK SUPPLIES. I MISS YOU TERRIBLY BUT AM ALSO GLAD YOU'RE IN A RELATIVELY SAFER PLACE. ONE OF US MUST SURVIVE ALL THIS.

〉〉〉〉〉▶▶▶●●●●

The space exploration initiated in the 20th century had pretty much come to a standstill with the secessionist move, although the early part of the 21st century had seen a boom in vanity flights for tourists as well as a variety of unmanned flights throughout this solar system and a few probes sent out beyond. The question continued to be: is there life beyond our planet and if so, what kind? Attempts were made to send a variety of unmanned scanner probes to Mars and Jupiter's moons, with plans for a manned flight to Mars toward the end of the 21st century, but chaos at home put all these plans on hold after the middle of the 21st century. The Moon, close as it was, continued to attract attention. At first it was limited to exploration, with the U.S. and Cali-Texas jointly exploring one side of the Moon with support from Europe, and China and Russia, that became the Ruso-Chinese Confederation, exploring the other side. As far as lunar exploration, it had in fact not attracted much interest really since the Lunar Orbiter Program of 1966 and '67 and the Apollo Missions of 1969 and early '70s. Then came the Lunar Reconnaissance Orbiter of the early 21st century. Unmanned flights to the Moon with an eye for locating appropriate colonization sites started up again in the late 21st century and plans for establishing a new type of lunar space station from which future space exploration could be initiated also began attracting more attention.

With the election of Villar-Gómez as President of Cali-Texas in 2090 and in view of the Ruso-Chinese lunar projects, there came a new impetus to re-initiate plans for establishing colonies on the Moon. With a Ph.D. in astronomy, Villar-Gómez saw the exploration of the Moon as a solution to several problems: ecological and labor. To carry out these projects, what was especially urgent was the discovery of appropriate lunar sites for the establishment of disposal sites where we could deposit radioactive material and other waste products that were no longer disposable on Earth. New manned flights were sent after 2095 and within a period of twenty years a range of experiments on the Moon as well as on Earth led to the finding, limited though it was, of lunar water in shadowed craters. We no longer had to depend on its being brought up from craters at the south lunar pole where caches of frozen water had been hidden away for billions of years. There was also a great deal of interest in the mining of certain minerals already detected in the 20th century, minerals which were potentially new energy sources. While the first outpost was slated to be a waste dump, the second was supposed to be a mining site. A third site would be laid out for the establishment of a research laboratory to establish an observatory for the study of distant galaxies, set up accelerators to investigate the long-term impact of space on the human body, and perhaps, given the right lab conditions, to develop a unified theory of physics. It was the observatory that interested me especially, but I was never invited to participate in that research. In time, they thought back then, perhaps by the end of the twenty-second century, all three Earth powers would establish some 20 colonies on the Moon.

( ))))) ▶ ▶ ● ● ● ● ●

— LISTEN UP, RESCHIC: YOUR JOB HERE AT THE DONOVAN TRAINING FACILITY IS TO CORRELATE AND SYSTEMATIZE ALL THE INFORMATION TO BE FOUND IN THESE FILES. ANY DISCREPANCIES ARE TO BE REPORTED TO ME, BUT FIRST VERIFY WHETHER IT'S A glitch in the computer, on the server, or in the transmission of the data. You're the computer expert here, but make sure your analysis is accurate and completed by the specified time. Now get to work. And when you're done, take a look at these other computer programs; they don't seem to be working out as planned.

I felt like a total failure. here I was in a prison, even if they called it something else. Training facility, my eye! Gabriel was in Brazil and who the hell knew how he was doing. My parents and Lupita were still stuck at the Reservation. Me and my big plans to help start the revolution! Fortunately, Ricardo had gotten away. He had to play it safe, lie low for a while, go on with his studies; he had to; no tenía otra.

)))))) ▸ ▸ ▪ ● ● ● ●

Right. Right. The commons was already set up when we arrived. Mucho antes. At first they were suspicious of our wanting to join them, even though, Guamán the Elder, whom we had met at a meeting in Iguazú, had recommended our joining the group. Rubén Guzñay was especially suspicious since we were coming from Cali-Texas. Even after he learned how we had escaped from the Moon, he was wary of our being here, until we began working the fields with them, helping them set up a clinic with Betty providing healthcare, and Tom and I began teaching in the evenings, after we had cultivated the garden. Leticia and Maggie helped set up a satellite dish that allowed us to communicate better with other communities in this hemisphere and in Mexico, and Frank and I developed protocols for non-commercial internet connections with other indigenous groups throughout the Americas and eventually in the Pacific Rim as well. Still, being and feeling accepted took a long time and it was only after you were born and Tom and Betty had adopted Guamancito that it became clear to some of the leaders that we were here to stay. As our Quechua improved we also made friends with a variety of groups, especially women's groups led by Lorenza Guzñay. Eventually some from our group, especially the miners, moved to the outskirts of the commons, on the road to Macas, but Frank and you and me stayed and became part of the community.

Frank and I arrived twelve years ago and you were born here almost ten years ago. Yes, Pedro, I know. Your birthday's coming up. This is your home, the place that will define you in some crucial way, in the way that place makes us what we are, the source from which you gain particular insights and perspectives. Space is formative, and when you grow up and become an astronomer, Pedro, you will need to remember this alternative space in which you were born and recall always that space is a product of social relations. Right, you're right, I am talking about a different kind of space. Here, not outer space. You'll undoubtedly be involved in the production of new spatial relations, maybe —hopefully — even in outer space, on another planet, but I want you never to forget this particular place, our commons, and that it represents a rejection of everything that is hegemonic and dominated by capital relations. Maybe it'll serve as a model for you and others like you to build a new beginning elsewhere. For Frank and me, unfortunately, our space was also formative — all too formative— and there is no way we can continue living here without trying at least to change the particular conditions that make up our formative space back in Cali-Texas. My place, that Fresno Reservation, is at the root of all my struggles. But I will tell you more about that place another time, son, not today. You're falling asleep, I can see; yes, you are my spaced out little boy today. Duérmete.

)))))))))))

It took a while to bring the states and conglomerates on board for a joint space exploration project that would begin with the Moon. The project was to be unified at the level of technology, but locally each site could have its own corporate sponsor.

Despite the original plans, the first colonies established by Cali-Texas were not the waste dump sites, but rather mining sites, following the model set up by the Chinese, who were ahead of us by several years. The project involved the construction of sublunar pavilions as living quarters, and finding water and fuel sources. The planned establishment of gardens has still not materialized today on CaliTexas moon sites, but the Labs continue R & D work on that. Food sources still have to be delivered from Earth, some of it stays cryo-dried aboard mini-stations in moon orbit until requisitioned, at which point the cryod meals are sent down robotically to the surface by lunar landers. Following the Chinese model, by 2108 the first crew of Cali-Texas miners arrived at Crater Copernicus and set up in a nearby area, some 60 miles away, what would be called the Exo-Chev Mining Camp. This experience enabled the construction of the second colony, the research laboratory established in 2110. It was not till 2113 that plans for the CaliTexas Waste Dump were developed and the site selected for the construction of storage pavilions and bunkers.

    The main problem from the very beginning was always materials logistics. With the space craft in orbit, smaller shuttles were able to transport the colonists or miners and their supplies, but the construction of sublunar pavilions required heavy machinery as well as the transportation from Earth of tanks, siding, cement, and electronic equipment; this material was brought by the space ships. The monthly transport of waste deposits in tanks, on the other hand, proved to be an expensive proposition. To diminish the load on the ship, the cargo of tanks containing radioactive material was sent on a monthly basis by rocket from Earth, picked up from orbit by what we called space tugs, and brought down to low orbits, becoming lunar satellites that were eventually picked up by robotic landers launched from the lunar surface that brought the payload down by remote control to the surface of the Moon, hopefully, without crashing and compromising the load. It took a while before the system was perfected but after a few months the project was progressing.

Numerous attempts have been tried to develop new ways of launching ships, whether manned or unmanned, that do not involve several stages and prohibitive costs. What's being tested now is the creation of force-fields in particular areas, like Yucatán, Cuba and Northeastern Brazil, to neutralize the effects of gravity; the idea, of course, is to cut back on fuel costs and make transports more cost effective. If these attempts prove successful, it will be a technological breakthrough and revolutionize space travel.

· ·))))) ▸ ▸ ● ● ● ● ●

—Apá, why are we reslifers? Why do we have to live on the Reservation?

—Lydia, try to understand. When I was laid off, this was before you were born, Ricardo, your Mom and I lived in an apartment in Riverside, but when I was laid off and we couldn't pay the rent, they forced us to leave. We were out on the street with our belongings in boxes and bags. That's when they came for us and dragged us away, placing us all in one big cell with other families. Two days later we received what they called our "placement" orders. We were being transferred to Fresno, to this Reservation. This is where you and Lupita were born. But m'hija, don't despair. Some day we'll leave this place, I promise. De veras..

· ·))))) ▸ ▸ ● ● ● ● ●

At first robots were used to recover the payload, once it had landed, remove the waste tanks and load them on the rail flatbeds that had been assembled robotically to freight them to the pavilions and bunkers, where they would then be placed in containers. This involved identification of the different types of waste and the protocols to deal with them accordingly. What balled up and undermined everything was the constant breakdown of the robotic systems and the computers set up on the lunar surface to coordinate the process. As problems increased, it became evident that human workers or technicians were necessary as troubleshooters of both robots and computers. This in turn led to the recruitment of technicians and computer scientists that could deal with the logistics of this waste disposal. The use of robotic instruments for the most part meant that only a few Tecos had to be on hand, but these had to be trained waste management specialists. The contract called for techs willing to work on the Moon for four years; the private corporation in charge of the waste disposal would provide housing and meals and other basic necessities (including bedding, soap, deodorant, cigarettes, beer, wine, marihuana, morcaine patches and whatever other recreational drugs were needed; (by the middle of the 21st century drugs had been legalized; that, in itself, put an end to a number of problems, but I'll tell you about that some other time); the crews' salaries, including hazard pay, was to be deposited monthly at the Central Bank of Cali-Texas. Yes, yes, what Guamancito told you is true; coca was once considered an illegal drug in some places.

〉〉〉〉〉〉▶▶▶●●●●

O.K., I already told you, I think, that I was raised on a Reservation near Fresno. California's Central Valley had long ceased to produce anything; it was one of the first areas wiped out by the desertification process that started in the middle of the 21st century. Anyhow, Reservations were composed of numbered neighborhoods; each had a number of housing projects with an internal patio surrounded by rectangular buildings, each seven floors high. All streets had surveillance cameras and our faces were automatically recognized since Reservation entry and birth meant a residency card fitted with a computer chip that had all our information on it. We lived in neighborhood #23, on the third floor of a building that had a view from our kitchen window of the distant mountain range. My father worked in a maquila that assembled electronic equipment and my mother, after we were all over 5 years old, was assigned to work in the Reservation nursery.

My brother and I had bikes and we enjoyed riding them to the edge of the Reservation which was surrounded by razor wire that also separated one complex from another. We couldn't go beyond our neighborhood but within it we could walk or ride our bikes; each neighborhood had a small plaza, a mall with a movie plex, a clinic and a storehouse where you could requisition supplies and provisions. No money or scrip circulated in the neighborhood when I was young, but we had supply forms on line at the commissary. I spent over 15 years there, until my older brother Ricardo and I were chosen to attend schools that specialized in math and science outside the Reservation. We were then sent south to Los Angeles where we lived in a dorm while I went to school and Ricardo to college; when I graduated, I too was sent to the university; we could no longer see our families as they were not allowed to leave, but we could communicate and keep up with events on the Res through e-mail and by visphone. And then one day we joined organizers interested in supporting those planning to go on strike inside the Reservations. It happened about 4 or 5 years after Ricardo and I first left, when we were already at the university and had jobs working as assistants at a couple of R & D labs in SoCal.

〉〉〉〉〉▶▶●●●●●

"Compañeros, it is work that unites us and everything and anything that serves to divide us is to the benefit of the capitalists. What is clear is that there can be no strength in our movement as long as there are wageless workers, that is, slaves on the Reservations, because what are those Reservations but prisons? The people within the Reservations, our parents, brothers and sisters, cannot leave; they constitute an indentured labor pool, without rights, without freedom. While the corporations can use those workers without sharing with them any part of the surplus value they produce, our own salaries have

REMAINED LOW AND WE LIVE UNDER CONSTANT THREAT OF BEING LAID OFF AND HAVING OUR JOBS OUTSOURCED TO A RESERVATION. COMPAÑEROS, IT IS TIME TO PUT AN END TO THESE RESERVATIONS. ¡A DESALAMBRAR!"

⁂

The chaos produced by recessions and political turmoil in the late 21st century gave rise to the organization of new labor and student movements with some links to global movements against the New Imperial Order, especially in Latin America. The anti-NIO movement was also a response to the creation of class reservations that had been proposed even before the breakup of the United States, with the establishment of a police state. The creation of Cali-Texas didn't mean the end of plans for these Reservations, as some liberals had previously thought; in fact, just the opposite happened. These liberals had faith in working through the system and thought that as the members of the segregated racial and ethnic groups came to power, new structures would be established. But despite the fact that we Latinos long ago had become the majority population in the new Cali-Texas nation-state, we, along with blacks, Asians, Native Americans and poor whites, made up the majority of those put away in these Reservation camps after 2090 since most of us had no capital, no jobs, and no connections. It was Gabriel, your father, who first took me and Ricardo to a meeting of student workers who were uniting with service workers interested in organizing on the Res. Trying to coordinate our studies with our lab work and with union work complicated our lives no end and I even came to think that it might be a good idea to drop out of the university, but of course that wasn't an option, given my chola status. It would have meant going right back to the Res.

    The primary task of our student-labor group was organizing and supporting protests at the Reservations themselves, something that I felt that I would be able to do well since I myself had lived on the FresRes from birth to the age of 15. And as it happened, one Saturday our union organizers drove us up to the Fresno Reservation and with pliers we began to cut the razor wire fence and shouted to the people inside to step out of the enclosed area. Most of them didn't dare come out but hundreds did, especially young people, who jumped at the chance to run out to the barren fields. We made a number of campfires and ate hotdogs to celebrate what turned out, of course, to be no more than a symbolic act. Yes, hotdogs, can you believe that, Pedrito!

)))))))●●●●●●

— Apá, Amá, we're here, over here. We're here. Let me give you a big, big hug. Where's Lupita? Ah, there she is, gritando como siempre: "Lydia, Ricardo." Como has crecido, Niña. She's gotten tall, no crees, Ricardo? We can't believe it; we're so happy to see you. Are you going to join us? No, don't worry, Ricardo and I are not going to force you to come out beyond the fence. Yeah, I know, the tower. What you smell are hotdogs. Here, have one. We made them out there beyond the fence. Yes, we'll come by again before leaving. Vente ya, Ricardo. We need to get back. Vámonos ya.

)))))))●●●●●●

But Ricardo and I were not able to go back to see them again that day or any other, because five minutes later we were surrounded by the police and arrested. We spent two days in jail. Our protests and symbolic "defencing" and "freeing" of the Res workers across the state, unfortunately, had no impact, despite its being mostly a Latino-led government. What had already become all too clear was that skin color, race, ethnicity, and language were irrelevant to the President and his power brokers whose main objectives continued to be the accumulation of capital and the welfare of the NIO corporations, especially in view of the growing competition from China and Europe. Any illusions that we might have had that protests and demonstrations would put pressure on the state proved misguided. Villar-Gómez's protégé, the new President, Simón Perusquillo, also failed to put an end to the Reservations. Ultimately capital can undo any ties or links on the basis of race, ethnicity, language or color. Remember, Pedro, it's the system.

)))))) ▶ ▶ ▶ ● ● ● ●

Gabriel and I were already working underground with the anarchos but our graduate research was good and perhaps for that reason the University allowed us to attend a bio-engineering conference in Mexico City. By then we were living together and making plans for a future together, although we knew those plans would need to be postponed for a good while. We had political obligations as well as family and academic ones. The university put us up at a hotel near the new Convention Center in Mexico City where all sorts of projects were being discussed, including DESAL and nuclear plants all along the Mexican coasts. While the northern Mexican states had become part of Cali-Texas, the rest of the country was still "independent," but only in name. CaliTexas pretty much controlled the entire area all the way down to Colombia. Only Venezuela and Ecuador had resisted attempts to create an Américas Commonwealth. Bolívar must have been turning over in his grave, no doubt.

— What do you say, Gabo, like they used to say in the movies. Should we make a run for it?

— Oh, wouldn't I love to. We could try to reach Bariloche and Ushuaia in Tierra del Fuego. There we would undoubtedly find work, with our training, no crees?

— Yes, and I could focus on my astronomy and you could hook up with a bio-chemical lab.

— It is worth a try, now that we're here. It would be easy to hide among the population. We look like everybody else here.

— But what about our families? What about our struggle?

— I know, it's crazy to think we could leave them behind, make them subject to punishment for our escape. No, we can't.

— You have to admit It was a good idea, even if only for a few minutes.

— I have another one. Come sit with me and listen up. I was talking to this guy at our session who works for a cryogenics lab and he was telling me about cryonics and about our being able to get in as donors to freeze a little part of us. His father manages the lab.

— What are you getting at, Gabo?

— Well, the way things are going, we could end up dead at one of our demonstrations, if the police come in shooting. This way, whoever survives would have part of the other in a fertilized egg or two that we could safeguard frozen at this guy's lab. What do you say? We could go meet him during the lunch break and talk. Dime que sí.

༺ ༻ ༻ ༻ ༻ ༻ ༻ ༻ ༻ ༻ ༻ ༻

Most of us were convinced pretty early on that the new Latinoidentified nation-state would not bring about dramatic political changes, but I think we were not prepared for the draconian measures that followed to ensure our failure in fomenting any change to the new state territory. The truth is that we were totally crushed. Ever harsher repressive measures eliminated even symbolic protests; blinding of surveillance cameras, spray painting on walls, use of banners and signs, it all became a major crime under the anti-terror rubric. The new Cali-Texas thus proved to be just a more effective instrument of capital and the NIO. The subsequent conservatism that prevailed wiped out any attempts at even liberal reforms, some of which had at least been paid lip service under the U.S., like social security and free education. Health care benefits were wiped out except for minimal care within the Reservations, with all care privatized beyond minimal first aid.

  Of course the streets in the metropolitan areas were now clean, devoid of street people or trash. It all looked artificially sterile. Life went on behind closed doors and the underground luxury trains carried the wealthy to clubs, theaters, movie houses and shopping malls. For the most part, only commercial vehicles circulated on the freeways and streets, as did the workers; the skilled labor force and professionals transported on MagLev railways. Segregation became more and more visible as it became a two-tiered metropolitan site. From what we hear, since we've been here in Chinganaza, things have not changed; they've only gotten worse. Yes, that's why we have to go back.

〉〉〉〉〉〉▶▶●●●●●

All right, Pedro, you too, Guamán. Take your earpods off. It's time to return to your lesson. Space, that is, the universe, is made up of billions and billions of galaxies, each one with millions of stars, and planets that orbit each star. It appears that the universe is unending; in other words, it has no borders. What's more, it is always expanding. Will it one day contract and curve into itself? We don't know. Some even doubt it. The light of distant galaxies that reaches us across space after millions or billions of years seems to indicate that these galaxies are distancing themselves even more, suggesting expansion. That also implies that billions of years ago these stars were closer; they and the distance between them are the product of the Big Bang. No, you two can't call it "el gran pedazo." Come on, concentrate and quit laughing.

⋅ ⋅ ⟩ ⟩ ⟩ ⟩ ▸ ▸ ● ● ● ● ● ●

Those of us on the Left that survived the Cali-Texas purges (Can you believe I was only 19 years old then?) began again to organize, this time more solidly in terms of a global movement that synchronized local cells through alternative internet systems that piggybacked clandestinely on the worldwide communication grid. In this way we were able to reach even the farthest village in Peru and Brazil as well as some in Africa and Asia. I got involved with a small group at the university, but as time went on I found the group to be more academic and theoretical than involved in praxis. It had given up all thought of revolt or revolution and in fact most just pooh-pooped even use of the term "revolution" itself. It was then that Gabriel and I joined the anarchos, who continued participating in local protests and in small-scale acts of violence against the NIO global corporate offices, against the police and armed forces, against the transportation systems, and against commercial centers. We were especially interested in making a statement against property and enclosure. We were the urban Maquis, with our own brand of low intensity guerrilla warfare. Clearly we did not have the means or manpower, nor the weapons, to do anything else.

By then I was finishing up my first year as a graduate student, naturally on fellowship. Your uncle Ricardo was in his third year of graduate school. During the daytime I studied and taught, but in the evening I joined the others in my group in various types of actions until one day somebody in the group set us up. Someone tipped the police off as to where we would be that night. We were in the process of breaking windows at the headquarters of the Fuelamerica when the raid began; we were surrounded, hit with tear gas and tasered by laser pellet guns. Of the ten of us involved in that small action, eight were caught and jailed. Fortunately,

Ricardo got away. That was in 2123. I was 21 when I, along with Gabriel and the others, was sentenced to prison for terrorism and crimes against the state and against private property. Despite my big mouth, I was lucky. Others involved in similar protests often got much worse. The death penalty still applied to all terrorist convictions.

〉〉〉〉〉〉❯❯❯●●●●

It was Fresno, hot and dry. I took Lupita to the mall in the middle of the afternoon one day. It was supposed to be a treat. Lupita was around 8 then, just a kid, and I was 12, I think. Ricardo didn't want to go with us. He preferred to stay at home playing his video games. He always said those games were his lifeline. As we walked, I could see the 100-foot-tall tower with radar and highdefinition cameras straight ahead. I knew they were watching us; they always were. The cameras, set off by radar, beam high-quality images of targets to internal FresRes police as well as to the security stations five miles away in every direction. The Reservation was like a panopticon prison; from the tower they could scan the perimeter as well as every inch of the Reservation and see everything and everybody. They could also hear everything, if they wanted to. As we got to the mall, I could see two of Ricardo's friends working at one of the burger places; they had to work on the weekends because their father had tried to escape from the Reservation and their mother couldn't get enough hours of work to meet their needs, that is, to work off what they consumed. Their father was found dead four miles from the fence; no one leaves. Down another street I could make out a bunch of kids cleaning the streets. Any delinquency was punishable with work. As we walked into the movie mall, we showed our IDs and the doorman scanned them. That was how they kept track of our consumption and how much my father and mother had to work on a weekly basis to compensate the Reservation for our expenses.

There was a new kids' video just out that Lupita was dying to get. It dealt with dragons and witches. I could see down the hallway that the teenagers in the music room were all getting high. It was allowed, even encouraged, as long as it was consumed in designated areas, but in the end it did little to alienate the boredom that all of us lived with day to day. If you were too old for kids' movies, the only other thing to do on the Res was to get high; there was nothing else. We got Lupita's movie, our card was scanned, and scanned again when we went to the ice-cream place next door for a cone. Then we began walking back to our apartment. I looked up at the windows of apartments nearby to see if I could spot any of my girlfriends, but there was no one around. That meant only one thing; they had been taken to clean the offices of the Reservation directors; it was tough when your mother was a single head of household and there were several children to clothe, feed, and get an occasional video and ice cream for. They made you work on weekends as soon as you were 12. I felt I was lucky. Both of my parents worked. I often wondered what it would be like not having to live there, to be able to stray beyond the fence. I figured that I would probably just run and run and enjoy the empty space. I heard that not too far away there were trees and grass and even a river. I often wondered what our lives would be like in ten years. For sure in three or four years it would be decided for us whether Ricardo and I continued in school or went to work. As we neared our place, for some reason I kept thinking about how long it was going to take my dad to work off the two ice creams we had just had.

))))))))••••••

In the close to two years that I was imprisoned at the Donovan Prison in SanTijuana, the unemployment of techs and laborers in Cali-Texas increased substantially, even as the corporations accumulated larger and larger profits. Two percent of the population was made up of billionaires and 50% lived below the poverty line, and that was in the good times. To ensure that the destitute were not lining up along the main thoroughfares, the number of Reservations increased dramatically as the government of CaliTexas decreed that all new unemployed individuals would also be sent to the Reservations unless at least one family member had a fulltime job and made enough for the housing and basic needs of the family. Understandably, this new policy led to more protests and street actions. At this stage, as demonstrations and disturbances increased, endangering the economy, the government initiated its Labor Corps. Under this program, the government could forcibly recruit any individual, male or female, who was unemployed and under the age of 50. Persons without university training would be trained as enforcers of so-called industrial management policies and sent to the thousands of factories established by NIO global corporations anywhere throughout the world. Employment with the Labor Corps also enabled the recovery of citizenship rights, denied to those living on Reservations or in prisons, reinstating as well entitlement to social services. These labor "managers" were sent primarily to Latin America, but some also served in sweat shops established within Cali-Texas, especially in the former northern Mexican states. "Managers" or "Mániches," as they were also known, were all considered sellouts serving as lackeys; for everyone knew that policing one's fellow workers was akin to being a traitor to one's class since a manager's main task as controller was to inform on non-compliant workers seeking to throw a monkey wrench in the system. Mániches were vendidos, basically, on the lookout for anyone who protested conditions and salaries, or initiated slowdowns.

We know also that the universe has many histories, that is, that it undergoes many changes and faces many possible turns or possibilities, for example, the creation of galaxies. In the universe what operates is the Uncertainty Principle. Our lives seem to run on the same principle, but that's philosophy not science, Pedrito.

〉〉〉〉〉▶▶▶●●●●

The eight of us who were charged with being subversive anarchos were all sentenced to 10 years in prison, but the state, noting its previous "investment" in our education,— we were after all university students with different types of skills— offered us an out; we were given the option of joining the Labor Corps, working for the global corporations that were interested in attracting high skill technicians to send to some of the more remote areas where middle class university graduates were generally reluctant to go. They were especially looking for techs for research and experimentation in biology labs as well as informatics or computer science, primarily related to the data services for their worldwide satellite surveillance networks. The idea of working for NIO corporations didn't sit well with me. There was no avoiding the fact that it meant working for the enemy. Gabriel, my partner, was a bio-chemist; he preferred being sent to the Amazon to work in the laboratories established there for the creation of synthetic organ tissue, involving the Caoutchoua Brasiliensis, which had been used centuries earlier for the production of rubber. The indigenous populations of the Amazon that had fled the deforestation and were now reduced mostly to living on reservations in the western part of Brazil, near the Peruvian and Ecuadorian borders (Ecuador by then had reclaimed part of its Amazonian region), served not only as laborers and service workers but also as guinea pigs for the testing of artificial organ tissue by surgeons working at the bio-pharma labs. Gabriel felt that he might learn something useful at that lab and hoped he could make contact with Latin American anarchos we knew of while he was there; really, anything was preferable to rotting in prison for ten whole years.

    Myself, I chose to stay in prison at Donovan. A year later, the same bio-pharma laboratory that had recruited Gabriel had him executed on site, alleging that he had destroyed valuable lab resources and tried to foment an uprising among the Indians living in the camps. As a private contractor no trial was required and no appeal was possible.

    When I received the encrypted e-mail that one of Gabriel's fellow lab assistants sent me through a safe channel, I fell into a total state of depression, but there was no choice but to keep working. Five days a week for 10 hour shifts I either worked out kinks in computer programs or processed e-information provided by a variety of state offices; the processing work that had previously been outsourced to the Caribbean was now being done in prisons, where the labor cost nothing, except our lodging and meals. It was tedious work, and I was bored, although once in a while I would get a glimpse of some research projects in the works. I learned, for example, that the government was hard at work on two related memory projects. One involved purging memory on all digitized materials that were publicly accessible. This called for revising historical accounts not favorable to the Cali-Texas government. It was an enormous project that required outsourcing to various points in the south; huge processing centers or labs were established in Mexico and Central America to purge data banks, blogs, and even private accounts. As a computer tech I was asked to work on improving the "search-and-revise" protocols and commands. This purging was ironically linked to another project initiated to help restore memory in patients suffering from dementia. The same algorithms that were being used to "search and revise" digitized data were also being used to access implanted nodules in patients, searching their brains digitally for information. Developing nodules that converted brain waves to digitized data had been the brainchild of a late twenty-first century neurologist, Neda Chomsky. In both projects I was but a low-level prison technician with the ability to code, decode, and recode any computer language then known to the field, and, let's face it, no more than forced labor, a worker that had to do as she was told. Still, finding out about these projects was one of the few things in prison that had the effect of both horrifying me and giving me hope that one day what was being purged could be accessed and restored.

Access to computers, restricted as it was, sometimes proved useful. Once in a while I could even tap special government files, as long as I camouflaged the search. At first my constant query was: what else is the government up to? Perhaps by being in prison I could learn something about the inside workings of the beast. But, as time went by and Gabriel's death sunk in, I became more and more cynical and, in some way, began to give up on my hope for any kind of a better future. Perhaps social change wasn't even possible. Perhaps there really was no alternative and capitalism would rule forever and we would all live and die on our Reservations and in our prison cells. Gabriel's death cemented my depression. I didn't even want out anymore, just to be done and over with it all. Basta ya, I said to myself more than once.

)))))))))

— Lydia, a ten year sentence is a long time. I can't spend my best years in this prison. You know I was almost ready to graduate and now this opportunity to work in Brazil is giving me hope. This project is at least related to my field and I'll gain some experience and be part of a research team, instead of rotting away in here behind these walls. Come with me to Brazil, Lydia. They need all kinds of experts for this project, and it pays.

But I didn't go with Gabriel. I regretted it a thousand times after he left. Although in prison we seldom were able to see each other, we continued to communicate electronically. Later when he was killed, only eight months after he arrived in Brazil, I'd spend my nights wondering if I could have done something to save him, if I had been there. Probably not. I would probably have been killed as well. But at least my Portuguese was better than his. Would that have helped? "Vou-me embora pra Pasargada," Gabriel would say laughing.

···)))) ▶ ▶ ● ● ● ● ●

I was feeling down and desperate. It was then that I heard about the waste management program recruiting technicians to go to the Moon. As part of the waste disposal project, these techs would be in charge of all computerized mechanisms, including the robotic instruments, the drills, the construction of the sublunar pavilions and bunkers, the railways for transporting the materials on the lunar sites, and the recovery of aerial rafts in orbit. The Moon bases required a variety of sophisticated computer programs for maintaining the artificial gravity in all facilities, as well as the oxygen level, the energy modules to produce electrical power and extract water, etc., etc. Some of the Tecos were responsible for the operation of robotic equipment and instruments but at least a couple, with advanced training in informatic systems were responsible for the programming and recoding of the computerized systems, in cases of failure, as the systems often broke down and had to be rebooted or, at worst, reprogrammed. They told me that if I accepted, my prison sentence would be reduced to the almost two years served plus four years service on the Moon, after training. I had no reason to live or stick around, so I signed up. Besides, I knew it was my one chance for space travel.

  What made the idea even more attractive was the thought of being paid for my work; a check would be deposited into an account in my name and my parents'. I let my parents know, and told them to use the money to buy their way out of the Reservation. Those who could demonstrate that they had enough funds to rent a place and live off the Reservation and become - in their words - "self-sufficient," could petition to leave. My father had been a tile setter by trade, but had left that job to work in construction with a company that went bankrupt during the recession, leaving him unemployed and unable to pay the rent for two months, like I told you. Right. Exactly. That's when he, my mother and brother Ricardo were sent to the Reservation, and that's how Lupita and I were born there.

))))))))

IN PRISON I BECAME USEFUL TO THE ADMINISTRATORS BECAUSE OF MY HIGH TECH TRAINING, ESPECIALLY WITH COMPUTERS. I COULD FIX ANYTHING THAT BROKE DOWN. WHEN THINGS WERE GOING WELL WITH THEIR COMMUNICATION SYSTEM, THEY MADE ME HELP WITH OTHER DUTIES, USING THE COMPUTER TO ORGANIZE DATA FILES, INPUT INFORMATION AND SUCH. SOMETIMES I HOPED THINGS WOULD BREAK DOWN SO THAT I COULD DO SOMETHING DIFFERENT. BUT AS I WORKED I FOUND THAT SINCE I WAS LEFT ALL ALONE IN MY CUBICLE, I COULD TAP INTO NUMEROUS FILES, EVEN SECRET POLICE FILES, ONCE I FIGURED OUT HOW TO MASK THE REQUEST. THAT IS HOW I FOUND OUT WHO HAD BETRAYED US AT THE FUELAMERICA CORPORATION DEMONSTRATION, THE PERSON THAT LED TO OUR BEING SENTENCED TO TEN YEARS IN PRISON FOR ACTS OF TERRORISM.

WE HAD BY THEN BEEN INVOLVED IN SEVERAL AGIT-PROP TYPE ACTS, TO CALL ATTENTION TO THE RESISTANCE OF THE ANARCHO MAQUIS, KNOWING FULL WELL THAT WE DID NOT HAVE THE POWER OR ORGANIZATION FOR A FULL SCALE INSURRECTION. BUT IT WAS IMPORTANT THAT PEOPLE BE MADE AWARE OF OUR WAR OF POSITION, OF OUR CONTINUED STRUGGLE AGAINST THE POLICIES BEING IMPLEMENTED AGAINST US. OUR MAQUIS LEADER WAS JUAN GÓMEZ AND IT WAS HE WHO FIRST SUGGESTED THE FUELAMERICA CORPORATION HEADQUARTERS "ACTION." THAT night we planned to break windows, break open the doors and spraypaint signs on the walls calling for an end to Reservations and the police state. Gómez too had been picked up that night but for some reason was not sentenced with the rest of us. We figured that as the leader of the group he was probably going to get an even harder sentence. I did not think about him again. But here I am, one day, snooping into police files and I find that Juan Gómez had been in their pay, reporting on political resistance activities. I could have strangled him. How to get the word out to those still agitating on campuses and elsewhere became an obsession for me. Gabriel was dead by then and I felt that Gómez in some way had condemned him to that particular death, by betraying us. But there was no way to communicate with anyone. I could receive all this information in prison, including information on Gabriel's death, but was unable to transmit anything out; all outmail was blocked except what was inspected by the prison surveillance firewall. It was when I signed up for the Moon trash-tech duty that I was taken out of prison and placed with the other trainees at the space center. Like them, I had access to various communication systems. The fact that these were also surveilled was not as important as getting the word out. One thing for sure; I knew I had to contact my former roommate Cecilia; we had roomed together before Gabriel and I started sharing a room at the same complex where she lived. Cecilia was part of our anarcho Maquis group but had been ill the night of the FuelAmerica action. She had insisted on coming but after I checked her temperature, Gabriel and I made her stay. That's why she was not in prison. Contacting her was less difficult, but I had to recall codes that I had not used in over two years. Cecilia and I had our own names for people and words to indicate "danger," "treason," or "trap." I was finally able to

CONCOCT A MESSAGE, LETTING HER KNOW AS WELL THAT I WOULD BE LEAVING FOR THE MOON. BEFORE WE SHIPPED OFF SHE WAS GRANTED A VISIT. WE MET AT THE SPACE CENTER AND SHE CONFIRMED WHAT I HAD ALREADY INTUITED. GÓMEZ'S BODY HAD BEEN FOUND RUN OVER BY A TRAIN IN SAN DIEGO COUNTY. I HAVEN'T HEARD FROM CECILIA SINCE THEN, BUT IF SHE IS STILL ALIVE I HOPE TO SEE HER AGAIN WHEN WE HEAD NORTH.

))))))▶▶●●●●●

On Team Four I was the only ex-convict; the other six were unemployed technicians, recruits who preferred to go to the Moon rather than be sent to a Reservation. The seven of us included three Latinas (Leticia, Maggie and me), two Asians (Chinese-Mexican [Frank], and Filipina [Betty]), and two Blacks (Jake and Sam). As native Cali-Texans we were all pretty much bilingual. There were four women and three men. It was the first time that women had been sent up as part of the Waste Management crew. After six months of training with a former lunar Teco who had been part of Team One on the Moon and who trained us regarding adapting to the lunar environment, we left the Cali-Texas space station in Yucatán and, once in orbit around the Moon, transferred from the ship to a lander or shuttle; we landed on the 5th of March, 2125, in Oceanus Procellarum, an area made up of 2 million square miles on the west zone of the nearest lunar area, with respect to the Earth, that is. Right up there, more or less. The landing area was full of craters, elevated areas with mountains and low, valley-like areas, carpeted with what looked like fine dust or perhaps lava, as well as rugged areas, rocky and sometimes terraced. The Cone Crater was our destination. The seven of us were the fourth team to arrive since the first waste disposal team had landed at the beginning of 2113. The previous teams had already left, but Team Three was still there when we arrived and they provided us with necessary status information on what the work involved before returning to Earth. One of the departing Team Three members was Frank's older brother, Peter, whom he hadn't seen in eight years since Peter had re-enlisted after his first four-year contract ended; both were really happy to see each other. There was to be a five-day overlap between our arrival and Team Three's departure on the same craft that had brought us up. In addition to the seven of us there was one other person at the Moon base, Bob Cortés, the person in charge of all site monitors and Earth communications, who had extended his contract twice and planned to stay another four years.

⁂

Yes, Pedro, you were named after your uncle Peter. Here, look. In this photo you can see where we were. The base camp, like the pavilions, were underground and all you can see are the tops of the roofs. And yes, we had electricity at the base camp; the sunlight was a source of solar power. Here's another one closer up. Right, they had to be subterranean to withstand the solar storms of high energy particles. OK, OK, sublunar, Little Mr. Know-it-all. While Earth is protected in these cases by its atmosphere and its magnetic field, the moon doesn't have anything like that. The problem of high levels of radiation and the solar winds of subnuclear particles required these constructions, and of course, the special suits that we had to wear. Scroll down and you can see a photo of the White Valley without rocks or hills or canyons that we saw as we were landing on the moon. It was a two and a half day trip. Once we began getting closer to the surface of the moon we saw the edge of the Cone Crater and the gigantic canyons and faults on the surface. The soil was dusty, but it wasn't a fine dust but rather more like jillions of tiny marbles, crystallizations of a previous stage. The moon is a stunning and scary sight. Night lasts 14 days of ours and the day is equally long. And the temperature. God, it can get cold, reaching -279 degrees Fahrenheit, that's below zero, and in the daytime it can climb all the way to 245 degrees F. Although the spacesuits were set up to allow us to function in extreme conditions, we knew that it was risky to work outside above 175 degrees F or under 100 degrees below zero. That meant that we could only work on the surface at certain hours of the day and night with our suits on, of course. We also had monthly quakes that were detected by our instruments but generally not by us Tecos. Once in a while we felt them, though. We also had meteor showers the size of grapefruit at least once a month and of course smaller ones were everyday events. You'll like this one; here is a picture of a meteor that fell shortly after we arrived. We nicknamed it "el huevonazo."

〉 〉 〉 〉 〉 ▶ ▶ ● ● ● ●

The first Cali-Texas Moon mining camp was established around 2108 at Copernicus Crater. The project involved in perforation and extraction of minerals would prove very profitable for 3M, Moon Mining Management Company, that recruited and sent the first miners for one-year and later, to six-year stints. They had already extracted titanium and were finding other valuable minerals as well. Their success led to the establishment of several other mining sites and in fifteen years there were already around 200 lunar miners in different mining colonies on the moon, named according to the NIO corporation sponsoring them: Bechtshell, Halliburtex, Exochev, Boelockeed, etc. The nearest mining colony to us, the Exochev mining camp, had some thirty miners; it was the third team to arrive there and was having limited success. The Chinese had also established a mining colony on the Moon, on the far side, since 2100, and the European Union had a colony somewhere, I think, between the Chinese camps and the CaliTexas camps. The Chinese and the European camps were involved in mining but also in doing research for space exploration. By the time we arrived in 2125 there were some 2,000 people on the Moon, all told; each colony or base was independently organized, but the three Procellarum Cali-Texas bases, including the laboratory, the waste disposal site and base, and the mining camp were centrally connected through the lab and not too distant from each other. The rest of the lunar colonies, on the other hand, were distant from one other, but the mag-shuttlettes could cover the 200 to 500 to 1000 miles in short periods of time.

    A few months after we arrived, your father Frank and I had mastered the routine. We were glad that members of Team Three had been there to teach us the ropes, although it was not too complicated to learn what needed doing and carry out our duties. Each of us had a particular assignment. It was best to work in the mornings, that is, the first hours of the lunar day, when the temperature ranged between -50 degrees and 180 degrees F. At noon, that is, after 6 or 7 earth days, when the temperature climbed to between 200 and 245 degrees F. we stayed at the underground base; we had a laboratory there where we could work. Since the lunar day lasts 14 earth days, it took us some time to get used to the schedule; it meant sleeping during the day and very little during the first 6 days, to take advantage of the temperature; then we would spend days and days at the camp because working outdoors meant heavy consumption of oxygen, and since we often had to travel to distance sites, it was best to go out when the temperature was neither too high, nor too low. In time, after we got to know each other, we spent a good deal of time talking, mostly discussing political and economic issues. I also gave some classes on basic programming and troubleshooting and such. We were all also into music, popular music, especially 20th and 21st century music that we had brought along with us. And reading, of course.

    We each had a text-pad that could include up to 5000 titles or readings. Before leaving for the Moon I requested 3000, a third in astronomy and physics, a third in world literature, and a third in history. Those long, long nights were spent reading, with music in the background. I'll have you know that in the two and a half years that we were on the Moon I went through all the Literature and most of the history. Most of the science readings were texts I had used in college but wanted them with me in case it was necessary to do a quick review. In fact I brought the text-pad back with me. I'm leaving it for you so that you can do some of the reading as well. You're almost 10 years old and I think it's time that you got into some of that world literature that I love so much. It goes back to Greek myths and plays, pre-Columbian indigenous poetry, African oral stories and on up to 22nd century literature. The pad also includes a number of detective stories, where you become the detective and solve your own cases, as well as some literary games where you write your own short stories.

◦)))) ▸ ▸ ▸ ● ● ● ● ●

My father was born in Texas but grew up in California. Because he still had family back in Texas he used to go there in the summers. I remember that he said there had once been free movement in the Southwest and that all it took was having enough money to take a bullet-train, a plane, or have your own car. The way he talked, you could tell He loved the Southwest landscape, driving his old car through the deserts, the mountains, the hill country in Texas, the Texas Valley, the New Mexico scenery, and especially along the California coast. Evenings in Fresno when it was not too hot we would sit outside and he would tell us about his trips across the Southwest. It all sounded rather surreal to us, being able to move about with a certain degree of freedom that we certainly did not know on the Reservation. What had happened? According to my Dad, there had been a lot of poverty then too, but the government had been too concerned with military and territorial issues to focus on internal matters much. It was after Cali-Texas became the hegemonic power allied to China that things changed drastically. New policies were implemented and the Reservations were built. That's how my parents ended up in the Fresno Reservation. My father never returned to Texas and now that he's much older and finally got out of the Reservation, thanks to Ricardo and me, all he wants to do is live with my Mom in North SanTijuana, as far away from the Reservation as he can and tend his garden, while he waits to meet his grandson. Yep, that's you. You're going to like your grandma and grandpa, Pedro. That I do know.

〇))))) ▸ ▸ ▸ ● ● ● ●

One of the things that I found most impressive was seeing the Earth at night. It really did look like a whitish-blue marble in the sky. At the base was Bob Cortés, the communications specialist who had been there since 2117, like Peter, having come with Team Two, and although he was not too familiar with all our tasks, he was able to give us some pointers that facilitated on the job learning. He too was a computer techie but seemingly not involved with the camp jobs. He was in charge of communicating with the Lab, monitoring our movements and messages on the lunar surface, ensuring that we returned back to the base after our assignments, procuring supplies as they were sent to the Lab but mostly scheduling shipments.

When on shift, after breakfast we would don our suits in the loading bay, make sure all our equipment was in working order, and go to our respective sites. We were all equipped with ocular implants to see at night and through the moon dust storms as well as with implanted transmitters and communicators or nano-nub (network unit bits). Nubs, we called them. Whatever we saw or heard could be picked up on a monitor back at the station unless we purposely blocked transmission by the nubs by messing with the powerpack on our suit sleeves. As far as we knew the implanted sensor functioned like a camera/radio, but we did not know that it could also transmit images, as we later learned. The powerpack had to be periodically recharged and it was fairly easy to remove and re-install. On work days, Frank and I would leave the base on our jeep. There were four jeeps at our camp base. No, they were not really jeeps, but they functioned like jeeps, with thick tires and inset metal wheels that allowed us to travel far from the base. The Rovers that had been used in earlier explorations of the moon had been replaced by these jeeps that could reach a velocity of 25 miles per hour, powered by battery packs. Our job was to inspect the new excavations and the construction of pavilions with six to ten bunkers each, with the capacity for the installation of six large containers within each bunker. Each tank was marked according to type of waste product and placed in a specified bunker.

    Of course, Pedro, our underground base was cabin-pressured. We didn't need to wear our spacesuits inside. The base was actually much like a cabin, a quonset hut so-to-speak. Small but with enough space for a com-center with an adjoining cubicle for Bob and towards the back seven additional cubicles, one for each of us with a bunk bed, lamp and small table. Yes, Pedro, we each had a mini-WC, no, no toilet paper, but we did have moist wipes that we used for everything, even "bathing," if you want to call it that. Once we had our spacesuits on we'd go to the loading dock, close the door securely behind us, climb some stairs and go outside. Our tools were in an attached shed by the door, securely clamped down with the shed door locked; we could open it with a code. A metal frame extended to the left of the shed where the jeeps were tethered, yeah, like horses. I see you've been watching those old westerns, verdad? A chain and wheel brake ensured that the jeeps would not move around.

    O.K., I'm getting to that… Your father, my MexicanChinese partner from Calexico, was a geologist, well, actually an unemployed geologist, before he signed on with the moon project. I, on the other hand, was a math, computer science and engineering student and an ex-con. Really. We were the inspectors and resident computer gurus at the Cone Crater site. Our background enabled us to make recommendations on perforation sites, the construction of the pavilions and sublunar vaults, and the designation of bunkers per pavilion. Frank and I also were in charge of fixing any glitches in the computer programming of the pavilions or the robotic mechanisms. We functioned a bit like supervisors, but we tried not to play the part of bosses, but rather serve more like consultants that could be asked about programs or the use of particular instruments. We also helped at times with the loading of the flatbeds on rails and checked the railing system to make sure that it was in working order. These tanks and containers were heavy but with robotic cranes the lunar workers could lift them pretty easily since there is little gravity on the moon. The earth has six times more gravity than the moon, as you well know (I think I've told you that dozens of times, right?)

When we left base camp that day we felt an earthquake.

— Did you just feel what I felt?

— You bet. It's that the moon is getting closer to the earth and it's the gravitational attraction that produces these quakes.

— Someone's been reviewing the moon manuals that we got. Chin, what's that ahead? It looks like a dust storm, like the kind they have in Arizona and Texas.

— Oh, yeah, it's a sand storm all right, but more like a marble storm. Strap in tight. You better hang on tight to those jeep handles.

〉〉〉〉〉▶▶●●●●●

My brother Peter and I were raised by my grandmother in Calexico. I was about 5 when my parents went to work at an uncle's restaurant in San Francisco to keep the family from being sent to a Res. My family came from a farming and gardening past but by the middle of the 21st century all that ended; their lands were taken over for the installation of lab facilities and waste disposal sites.

My great, great, great grandfather left California for Mexico in the late 19th century after Chinese immigrants began to be persecuted and gunned down in the mines and countryside. He left right after the 1871 Chinese massacre in Los Angeles. An argument between two Chinese men over a woman led to the death of a white man in the crossfire and that, in turn, triggered the massacre of some nineteen Chinese men. Some of the remaining Chinese stayed in Los Angeles but my great, great, great grandfather headed south, thinking of returning after a few years after things quieted down, but then the 1882 Chinese Exclusion Act put an end to that idea. He felt lucky to have gotten out alive, especially since he had been drinking and smoking at one of the very houses involved in the 1871 event. He first went to the Tecate farm and later moved further east to what in time became Mexicali. There he married a Mexican woman and continued working the land. A few years later, however, they moved across the border as Mexicans. By 1900, long before the new immigration regulations came into force, he had become a resident of the United States. The Ho family grew, 10 children; some eventually married either Mexicans or Chinese Mexicans, as my grandfather was not alone in his exile and return. Other Chinese men who had fled to Mexico later, joined him in Calexico. By the middle of the 20th century, with the end of the Exclusion act, new Chinese immigrants came to California and some of my great uncles married Chinese immigrant women, although, now that I think about it, most of my great aunts married Mexican men. In time, some of my great uncles moved to the San Francisco area and got into the restaurant business.

    My father, on the other hand, married a Chinese-Mexican woman; for a time they worked their vegetable gardens, selling produce till they were squeezed out, forced to sell after the state, arguing eminent domain, made them sell their lands as the state wished to put them to what they deemed more profitable use, that is for the installation of a series of pharma labs. By then most of our produce was coming from the South, anyway, and our little farms were expendable. My father tried getting a job in the labs, to no avail; only my mother was hired as a lab technician doing basic custodial work. The threat of being assigned to the Reservation became all the more real as my mother did not make enough money for a family of 5 children. That's when one of my uncles suggested that my parents move to San Francisco, where they could earn enough to send for our upkeep. We stayed behind with grandmother Ma, my mother's mother.

I was 10 years old when Peter graduated from high school. At 18 you either declared your intention to go to college or else you got a job. If you couldn't find one, then the Labor Corps would send you a draft notice. Peter, who loved working on his motorcycles and cars, did not have the grades; college was not in the picture for him. He knew that the Moon Project was looking for mining recruits and when other guys in Calexico signed up, he did too. He and his buddy Joe signed up together but they were not selected for the mining project but rather for the waste disposal project that by 2117 was ready to receive its second team. It was the recruitment ads and knowing about Peter and Joe that led my friend Tom (yes, your uncle Tom) to enlist a few years later; unlike Peter and Joe, he had two years of college and some geological background; perhaps that is why he was accepted by the mining project. Although Peter was 8 years older, he and I were close as he looked out for me once our parents left for San Francisco. He was my big brother, tall and strong, and I literally and figuratively looked up to him.

Perhaps that's why after my own graduation from college with a B.S. in geology and engineering and no job prospects, I too decided to join the Moon Program. I was assigned to the Waste Disposal Unit, although I was to be a consultant for the Mining Project as well. Obviously my programming and engineering skills were what proved especially attractive to the applicant selection committee. Most guys didn't make the list.

Your mother and I met at the Moon Project training session and we became good friends almost immediately, but it was only after our escape from the Moon that we realized that we couldn't live without each other.

Lydia and I will be leaving in a while, but remember this: You have family in Calexico, many cousins and aunts, and some in San Francisco. You are my son, Pedro Ho, and if you ever get the chance or if you should ever need to hide out, go to Calexico where your family will help you out. Now c'mere and give me a big hug.

⟩⟩⟩⟩⟩▶▶●●●●●

— Mom, what was it really like to live on the Reservation?
  — Well, you have to think about life there at more than one level. On the surface it was just a little town of cholos, except that it was surrounded by razor wire. Like a prison, actually, but not quite. We were able to work, study, live at our own place, and as long as we followed the rules, we were O.K. We self-disciplined ourselves and acted for the most part like nothing was wrong. But, if you broke a law or rule or protested, then you were disciplined harshly.
  — What's the worst thing that could happen?
  — I think I told you about the man that was shot trying to escape. One man was locked up within a cell for a whole year; he was fed and allowed to clean himself, but no one talked to him and he lived in isolation; when he got out he had gone crazy. Isolation can kill you; we are social animals and need to interact with others; if that is taken, we are no longer human.
  — But how did they make you behave a certain way? Wasn't it scary to think that you could do something wrong and end up separated from your family?
  — We knew about the guards in the towers and we knew we were always watched, but we didn't think about them. We went our own way, acting like nothing was wrong, knowing there were all these other agencies all around us regulating what we did, at work, at school, at the Res stores, and even at the churches, for those who went. We never did. You see, the state can use all kinds of strategies to keep you in check: coercion, self-discipline and all the agencies that affect your daily life.
  — Sounds bad, but did you ever talk about it at home or with friends?

— Oh, that we did, when we could. At home we'd whisper in the evening with music in the background so that their bugs couldn't pick up what was said or we'd write notes to each other, notes that we would then burn to ensure no evidence was left behind.
— How can people live like that, Momma?
— People have the ability to adapt, at least outwardly, but inside there is this need for freedom that never leaves you. It can become more important even than survival.`
— And that's why you're going back?
— Yes, son, that's why we have to return. And listen, if we don't succeed, the next generation, yours, will have to do the job.

>))))) ▶ ▶ ● ● ● ● ●

So, the problem of disposing of these non-recyclable or toxic materials had become a major problem by the beginning of the 22nd century, as I think I told you before. As a consequence, the Moon had in good measure become one huge waste dump. Some of the tanks sent were marked with a big red letter "R" and we knew that these were radioactive materials to be handled with care. As oil deposits had been depleted, the Earth began using more and more nuclear power to generate energy. At first the waste had been deposited on Earth in tanks lined with lead, but we all knew that in time these tanks would begin to deteriorate and contaminate the soil. After the Moon project was begun, most of these were now leaking and leaching, so they were unearthed, recovered with lead-lined material and shipped up to the Moon. Once there, storage pavilion doors were opened with a computerized code that led to a long tunnel that descended to a lower level. Along the lower part of the tunnel were bunkers, also with computerized entryways. The team members in charge of depositing the tanks or containers could open the bunkers, but once full and closed, only Frank and I could reopen the bunkers; in fact, once all the containers had been deposited in the bunkers or vaults, Frank and I would seal them shut. The radioactive tanks were arriving more frequently now and we were busy building new pavilions and bunkers. Storing these tanks in those subterranean bunkers, — O.K., O.K, sublunar bunkers, Mister know-it-all — was hard boring work, but better, I suppose, than staying in prison.

— What are you humming, Lydia?

— Oh, sorry. It's just that I forget that our nubs are connected and that you can hear what I say or hum.

—O.K. Hum a little more. Let me see if I can pick up some of it.

— "Against the wind. We were running against the wind."

— Oh, yeah, it's one of the oldies that Jake plays back at the base.

— Well, yeah, he plays it so often that now I've memorized it. Not only do I remember the songs but even the order in which they are played. You know how many times I must have heard that playlist?

When we arrived at Pavilion 10 and checked the logs, we found that three new containers of radioactive material had arrived and been deposited inside. At each pavilion entryway there was a monitor on which all deposits were inventoried. We decided to go in to check on the containers and ensure that the doors were properly locked down and sealed, if necessary, before heading out to examine the new excavations that were being worked on several miles to the north. Upon entering we discovered the containers on the flatbeds. Obviously the last shift hadn't had enough time to deposit them in the appropriate bunkers. I wanted to use the jeep to push the railcars down into the tunnel to deposit them in bunker #2 which was closest to the exit, but Frank insisted on first completely filling up the remaining space in bunker #1, so that we could then seal the door. My methodical Chinchicano partner had to do things just so. We had three containers and our logs indicated that bunker #1 could take one more; but when we got to the bunker entryway we found that the entry log indicated that the bunker was full. We figured there had to be some mistake since our records and the outdoor pavilion monitor did not match up with the bunker logs. We decided to check it out. Probably something was wrong with the computerized delivery systems in Pavilion 10.

》》》》》》》》》》》》

My mother loved to tell stories about the family, about our ancestors. This account I remember well.

— You see, we're descended from a valiant Indian leader, Pacomio. When the Spaniards came to California, they established missions as a way to occupy the land, that both the British and the Russians also wanted, and to pacify the Indians, who resented being displaced from their rancherías. Those Indians that came to the mission seeking food, clothing, and blankets were first baptized. Of course the Indians knew nothing about what was said in Spanish, but they went through the motions in order to get the gifts. Once baptized, however, they were considered neophytes and were not allowed to leave. They could either live within mission walls or within mission lands in their own rancherías, coming to the mission every morning for mass and breakfast before being sent off to the mission fields to work. If they tried to escape, going east to where the gentile or non-Christian Indians lived, the presidio soldiers went after them; they were hunted down and brought back in chains. The Indians often came to the mission as children, where they learned Spanish and sometimes how to read and write as well as a trade. But the Indians were not happy and in 1824, an ex-neophyte who had escaped from La Purísima Mission named Pacomio organized an uprising against the missionaries and presidio soldiers. Pacomio was a literate young man, acculturated and hardworking, but he wanted his freedom and that of all the other Indians. His plan included preparing weapons, mostly arrows and clubs, and organizing the Indians to meet when the word came down. But on the chosen day, his message to gather at the mission was intercepted. His rebellion was thus limited to the few Indians at the Purísima Mission; they were able to take over the mission but not before word went out to the presidio soldiers from Santa Barbara, who came the next day and attacked the Indians. Pacomio and his Indians were forced to surrender. The rebellion thus failed. Controlling communication is fundamental, Lydia. Remember that, M'hija.

— The Mission sounds a lot like the Reservation, Mom, and we're the Indians. What happened to Pacomio?

— He was taken prisoner; several of the Indians were hanged, but he, probably through the intervention of the missionary, was spared and put in the stockades at the presidio in Santa Barbara for a while, but then they let him go. He could not however go back to the mission nor to the gentile rancherías. He was sent up to Monterey, where he worked and married a girl from one of the ranchos, the daughter of an Indian woman and a mulatto who had come with the original settlers as a young boy. Pacomio became a respected member of the Monterey community. His children later married other Californios and one of his descendants was my father, Juan Robles. And you're right about the comparison, Lydia. Like for the neophytes, there's no way to get out of here unless you have help from the outside. Perhaps some day we can all leave. But then again, it may take a rebellion.

— So, we have a bit of Indian, Black and Spanish blood, right? What about Dad's background?

— You'll have to ask him. His story is a bit more complicated because his family started out in California, and then subsequent generations moved to New Mexico and Texas and eventually moved back.

— So, he's a Vallejo from California?

— Yes, he's descended from one of the illegitimate sons of the famous Mariano Guadalupe Vallejo with a Californio woman, whose Indian mother had come from Sonora in 1781 to establish the Los Angeles pueblo. The mother was then a young girl and once here married a San Diego presidio soldier and moved to San Diego, where she had several daughters. In the 1830s when Guadalupe was courting his future wife, Benicia Carrillo in San Diego, he spent time bedding two of the daughters of your father's Indian ancestor. He had a son with one daughter and a daughter with the other, illegitimate children that he never recognized. The mothers used the Vallejo last name nonetheless to name the children. Of course the children were fairskinned, like the father, and later married Californios. The daughter married an important man, Matías Moreno, who was the secretary of Pío Pico, the last Californio governor. The son, on the other hand, became a vaquero or something. You'll have to ask your Dad.

— Is that why my Dad's name is Mariano Vallejo? I'll be damned! You know, I'd never made the connection. What a history! Un vendido y un rebelde!

)))))))))))

Pavilion 10 had eight bunkers, with each one able to store 300 tons of radioactive waste. At the entrance of each pavilion, like I told you, was a computerized record of routing and capacity that enabled us to determine what bunkers still had space. The earth-sent containers were hexagonal and could be sealed; in each container we could stack a number of tanks, The containers were marked in terms of category and we were supposed to sort the tanks according to type of waste product. Our jobs as Tecos was to maintain the system operational. Our jeeps were equipped with cables, cells, laser drills, and everything else we needed to keep the computerized system up and working.

At bunker 1, the diagnostic checked out as fully operational but the entry logs didn't jive with our records. In fact, the bunker had already been sealed, although not properly. We decided to break the seal and inspect bunker 1. According to our records there were five full containers, but the entry log indicated that there were six. As we opened the entryway we saw that six containers were in place. Clearly someone had failed to enter the sixth one at the entrance. The un-logged container was the one in the back to the right. We noticed that it had been improperly placed; perhaps the container was not full since in some cases only a few tanks were placed within a larger container, and if there was still space, the container might not have been entered as full, as the Tecos awaited the next shipment. In those cases, however, the bunker was not sealed. We decided to check on the containers.

We first checked the records again for unaccounted deliveries but found none. Those delivering the tanks from the ships could seal the container once it was full but only Frank and I could seal the bunker or break any container or bunker seal for inspection as we were the only ones with the codes. Could one of the containers have been filled with some other material? Protocol was that the containers had to be filled to capacity since we were running out of space and not building bunkers fast enough to accommodate all the deliveries. We decided to open each one. All the front containers were full and properly sealed, even the one on the right. I started the back row at the left and Frank started on the right. I found the first two containers full and sealed. Fine. Frank found that the last one on the right was not properly sealed but before I went over to check it out with him, he made me a hand sign to hold off. Something was not right. The pressurized cover had been manually lifted; it was not properly closed; these covers could only be opened and closed with a code. The capacity log was also off line. Something was definitely wrong here.

    Frank and I had faced another odd situation a few weeks before and had been naïve enough to report it. It turned out to have been the negligence of two of our colleagues and they were written up and docked a week's pay. That had sparked problems among the Tecos and we had resolved to handle things differently next time we encountered a problem. Both of us decided to take a break and disconnect the com or nubs-monitor. We had approximately 3 minutes before an alarm would go off back at the base station, indicating that something was wrong. We examined the container and were able to manually open it despite the faulty closing. When Frank looked in, he almost fell back. I heard him gag, grabbed him and pushed him aside. I then took a look myself, gasped, and immediately closed the container cover, and dragged Frank outside. I felt nauseous but did my best to keep from throwing up. Frank looked stunned. After Bob came on the air and asked if we were all right, we connected the nubs, then disconnected the monitors again and went back into the vault to take a second look and seal the container. We then logged it in as full capacity before turning our monitors back on. I helped Frank back into the truck, closed up the bunker, and started toward the Pavilion 10 exit.

    We drove in absolute silence to the new site where Pavilion 13 was being built by the remote controlled drilling apparatus. Already the excavation had begun and the dust was whirling about. We decided to turn our nubs monitors off after sending the station a message that while inspecting the operation we would be off line, "dead," so-to-speak, for approximately five minutes. After sending the message and disconnecting the monitor, I turned to see Frank holding his head gear and crying. Our space suits made it difficult to hold him or comfort him. All I could do was hold him by the shoulders. It took him a couple of minutes to regain his composure.

What we had seen inside the container was beyond belief. Inside were the bodies, more like the skeletons, of Frank's brother Peter and other Tecos, probably the seven that had supposedly returned to Earth five days after we arrived to take their place. The top skeleton had a hole in his temple and a waste-tech shirt with Peter's name on it. The techs had been placed inside the container in a bunker marked full. But the entrance logs had not indicated that all the containers were full. Who could have killed them and why? Shortly after they left, we'd been told that Team 3 workers had arrived safely back on Earth. Frank had really enjoyed seeing his brother before Peter left with the others. Now it appeared that none of the Tecos had ever left. Could it be that no one who came up ever made it back? The implications were mind-boggling.

Weeks after their return, Frank had repeatedly tried to contact his brother back on Earth, to find out how he was doing, but the station uplink kept telling him that his brother Peter was not available, that he had already left the transport station to go to Calexico and had not reported in since his arrival. A few days later Frank had tried to contact Peter's best friend, Joe, who had returned with him, but he too was difficult to locate. When Frank tried to contact Joe's sister, she told him that Joe's locator said he had returned but that he hadn't contacted anybody yet. She thought that maybe he had taken a new assignment or had traveled to another station. They agreed that whoever heard from Peter or Joe would let the other know. After eight years up on the Moon base, her family was hoping to hear from Joe soon,

Frank had been a bit worried at first, but relaxed when he received the message: "All well down here. Will contact you soon. Been tied up. Take care. Peter." Now we knew he had received a fake message. What that also meant was that all our messages to Earth were monitored and clearly someone at the transport station had seen the need to put off suspicion by sending the message pretending to be Peter.

— Peter was so happy to be going home. He was planning on getting married and buying a place either in San

Francisco or Calexico with his savings. What do we do now, Lydia?

I too was stunned and didn't know what to say. We drove away from the dusty new construction site and made sure to reconnect our nubs. What had become clear to both of us and would gradually be clear to the rest of the Tecos on the station was that none of us were supposed to leave alive.

⁘ ⟩ ⟩ ⟩ ⟩ ▸ ▸ ● ● ● ● ●

How can I explain what it was like? I don't know that I can ever really convey effectively what occurred on the Moon? Will our son, Pedro, understand how that experience is related to what is happening today in the Ecuadorian Oriente and in Cali-Texas? How do you make sense of your life, those moments that are so like a distant past and yet not so different from what is going on today. Chingones and chingados, but on a totally different scale. I can't answer these questions; perhaps in the telling, in the writing, in the recollection of people, through memory, dialogues and scenes, it'll all make some sense to him, fragmented though it may be. The important thing is preparing him for what is to come, but in the meantime, perhaps these recollections will be of some help to him. I don't know.

Historicize, historicize, Frank says, recalling the words of an almost forgotten 20th century literary critic. And since he's better with words than I am, I will try to follow Frank's advice. Who says what and to whom is equally important. That's Maggie's take on it. I don't know whether to count on oral transmission or on writing. Like everything else, writing too is an act and in the end maybe it matters only to me. But, in the long run, I hope it will make sense and matter to Pedro as well, especially after Frank and I leave for whatever awaits us in Cali-Texas.

Back at our pressurized underground base we took off our spacesuits and went straight to our cubicles to rest up before our shift's meal. I could not lie still. I couldn't get the image of the desiccated dead bodies in the container out of my head. I went to look for Frank and upon entering his cubby disconnected my monitor. He was sitting on his bunk with his head in his hands, having a hard time breathing. I switched off his monitor and held him for a good while. At the station base we used to disconnect for 10 or 15 minutes and didn't get any grief for it, although technically we were only allowed to disconnect for 2 minutes, especially out in the field. The rooms had sound monitors so that even without our individual monitors on, the Lab, through Bob, could still pick up any conversation on the base. Often we communicated in sign language, inserting Spanish or caló words here and there. And for sure, no one wanted to be monitored while using the bathroom. That at least was one thing we'd managed to keep to ourselves. Nobody much cared about getting monitored when they paired off for whatever either, but going to the can was a different story. I decided to crank up the volume on some music, one of Sam's cells.

    —You like Rhythm and Blues, right? That ancient 20th century stuff!

    — Yeah, and old stuff, like jazz. I especially like Ray Charles. I guess I'm just an old fogey.

    — How about his version of "Yesterday." Just for you.

    — That one I really like.

While the music played, I began to whisper.

    — If they find out that we know, they will either deny it or remove us both. We'll just end up in one of the containers sooner.

    — This is looking really, really bad. We have to warn the others.

As a spatial fix for capital, the Moon project wasn't turning out to be too cost-effective, although at an ecological level the relocation of waste was definitely giving Earth some breathing room. The mining was promising, but the desired profitability from mining was off in the future. At a social organization level the Moon modules were turning out to be a recapitulation of Earth history. What was clear was that much like on Earth, on the Moon the Lab Director had the power to determine life and death.

There was much to think about. What was going on? Whose policies were being followed? Who was calling the shots? We went over all the procedures and possibilities. Frank and I were the only ones with the codes to open the bunkers and the containers, once sealed, we thought. But supposing someone else had access too, perhaps at our station, perhaps at the Lab, perhaps at the Com Center? What was clear was that the team of seven that had been at the base for the four prior years never made it home. Why not? The ship delivering supplies, high-tech instruments and crews, either to work in waste management or at the mining camp or at the Lab, had plenty of cargo space, after delivery, for the returning crew. We had arrived on one of those delivery ships and the same ship was supposed to have taken the previous crew back home. The returning techs had data that would have interested Earth, but nothing of a secret nature, nothing to kill for. The Communication Center and Laboratory had reported that all had gone well and that the ship had touched down back at Terrabase on time. That meant that everyone at the Com Center and Lab was in on it as well.

Returning crews were to report back to the waste management technician training center where some were contracted to train future Tecos; others had new assignments. What had really happened to the previous teams? Frank remembered that a member of Team 1 had been part of our training staff. Since I had arrived a week late, just out from prison, I had not met that trainer. Perhaps that team had made it back. Frank and I decided to check out the other pavilions, but first we needed to talk to Maggie and Leticia, our closest friends on the team since our training days in San Francisco. They had to be told.

· · ·)))) ▶ ▶ ▶ ● ● ● ●

THE ONLY THING THAT EASED FRANK'S PAIN WAS THE MARIHUANACOCA COCKTAIL THAT I CONCOCTED FOR HIM, BUT ONLY FOR A SHORT TIME. AS SOON AS IT WORE OFF, HE AGAIN DESPAIRED, AND WE COULD ONLY CONSUME WHAT WOULD WEAR OFF AFTER A FEW HOURS OF SLEEP OR ELSE WE'D RUN THE RISK OF FLOATING AWAY WHEN WE WENT OFF BASE. MAINTAINING OUR EQUILIBRIUM ON THE MOON SURFACE REQUIRED THAT WE BE SOBER AND ABLE TO USE OUR GRAVITATORS IF NEED BE. EVEN HOLDING HIM IN MY ARMS BEFORE WE FELL ASLEEP COULD NOT EASE HIS PAIN. THE LOSS OF PETER PRODUCED A DEEP SENSE OF LOSS IN HIM; IT WAS MORE THAN THE LOSS OF A BROTHER, IT WAS A LOSS OF FAITH IN THE STATE, IN THE SPACE CENTER BACK IN CALIFORNIA, IN THE LAB DIRECTOR, IN THE LAB RESEARCHERS, AND IN THE ASTRONAUTS. EVEN BOB WAS PROBABLY IN ON IT. I HAD LOST ANY REMNANT OF THAT KIND OF FAITH LONG BEFORE, BUT I UNDERSTOOD. PERHAPS SHARING THE INFORMATION WITH THE OTHERS WOULD HELP.

· ·)))) ▶ ▶ ▶ ● ● ● ●

Maggie and Leticia were part of the container delivery team. They were in charge of guiding the robotic landers or rafts to the landing strip on the Moon. Then, using hauling trucks with cranes they lifted the tanks from the rafts, brought them first to the storehouse next to the base runway and, from there, placed them on the railway flat beds. Their job after elevating their truck tire wheels and connecting the truck to the flat beds was to drive the cargo to the pavilions. After logging in the delivery they pulled the flatbeds inside the pavilion and stacked the tanks outside the particular bunkers where with the help of a robotic lifter, they took each tank and placed it within a container. Once full they closed the containers and sent us a message calling for inspection of the bunkers and sealing of the containers.

Back on Earth Maggie and Leticia were among the growing number of the "habitually unemployed"; they had found it hard to find work since robotic hauling, lifting and transporting had gradually replaced semi-skilled labor. Their sound tech and artistic skills couldn't get either of them a work contract for more than a day or two. Plus there was the other issue. Leticia's parents wanted nothing to do with the couple. Maggie's family wasn't in the picture either. For Maggie and Leticia the moon job had come at the right moment, just as they were about to get sent to the labor camps for those who hadn't secured a work contract on their own.

Frank and I re-engaged our nubs and went to meet the others for dinner. Our base, in addition to the individual cubicles, had a small kitchen-dining room where we heated up our rations and shared a beer or buzz. Maggie, the more intuitive one, sat next to Frank and asked if everything was all right. He nodded but sat in silence throughout the whole time. Someone piped in their music on the com and we sat listening to old twentieth century blues with Billie Holiday. When "Strange Fruit" came on, I suggested the four of us go over to my cubicle to play computerized card games. Both Leticia and Maggie looked at me funny, knowing full well that I hated those games, but, sensing something was up, got up to join us. The other three team members were busy playing computerized war games or betting on the outcome of a particularly heated football game back down on Earth, that was already a few days old.

In my cubicle I motioned to them to disengage their nubs as I disconnected my own monitor. I had previously tried unsuccessfully to disconnect a hidden sensor in my cubicle but finally found that jerry-rigging the cubicle's laser motion sensor caused interference if we jammed it up just enough. It was either that or put on the music really, really loud. One day, Frank and I had tested the disrupter by checking the monitors in Bob's office. All the monitors were accessible to him, and probably to the directors at the Lab as well. We were all pissed at the idea that even in our cubicles we could have a peeping Bob. Of course he claimed it was a safety measure. Sure. Luckily I had managed to find a way to disrupt the uploading mechanism, but we could use it only for a few minutes.

Anyhow, we disconnected our monitors, and I disrupted the sensor. Because Maggie and Leticia had picked up enough of the ASL and knew a bit of Spanish, we managed to convey that something was horribly wrong at one of the pavilions. We then made plans to meet the following day at the Pavilion 10 site before they made their way to Pavilion 12 to deposit the remainder of the last delivery of waste tanks.

〉〉〉〉〉〉▶▶●●●●●

— Mom, you sometimes talk about the cholos at the Reservation, but last week when we read about Ecuador's history, we learned about indians, cholos, mestizos and criollos. So, are your cholos, like the cholos in Ecuador?

— Well, not quite. The term originally referred to the urbanized indigenous population, to people who left the Indian community to work in town. These urbanized Indians began to change the way they dressed; instead of the traditional poncho, wool skirt, beads and bowler hats, they began wearing jackets, dresses and cotton skirts, and polyester chalinas. They also began speaking Spanish and living on the outskirts of the towns.

— Are the cholos then not pure Indians, Mom?

— After almost seven hundred years since the initial Spanish conquest, who's a pure anything? We're all mestizos of one kind or another, all mixed. But culturally and politically, like the members of our Chinganaza community, there are still groups that identify as indigenous populations, as Indians.

— What about the cholos in Cali-Texas?

— There's a history there too. My Dad explained once to us that back in the 19th century, the ex-convicts, men recruited from jails or prisons to come to Alta California as part of the governor's militia, were called cholos. Most were Indians but some were mestizos and mulattos. Later in the twentieth century, youth in the urban barrios who distinguished themselves by dress and haircut style were called cholos or vatos locos. As times changed, and Latinos became the majority population, with a large population of Latino-Blacks and Latino-Asians in the country, working class residents of all the barrios and ghettos became largely known as cholos. The term no longer applied only to the youth, but to the population at large.

— Are you a chola, too, Mom?

— Yes, for one simple reason. When the reservations were established around 2090 or a little bit thereafter, a new distinction arose. Those residents of barrios and ghettos with employment who could still afford to live in their homes or pay the rent became known as "la prole" or "los proles." Those who were unemployed and sent to the reservations, of whatever ethnic designation, became known as "cholos." Those of us living in the Fresno Res were the Fresno Res cholos. In fact we had a baseball team called the Fresno Cholos that beat the Modesto Res cholos in the finals when I was in middle school. My Mom and Dad took us all to see the game at the Res Diamond because it was free. My Dad said it was the first time an event had been free since we had moved there.

— So, is cholo a derrogatory term, Mom?

— Well, Pedrín, it is generally used to put us down, but to adapt the words of Mariátegui, a 20th century Peruvian writer, if as indians or cholos we have been oppressed, it will be as indians or cholos that we will rise up. With the support of the proles, of course. And that, m'hijo, is what we intend to do.

〉〉〉〉〉♦♦♦●●●●

Maggie and Leticia were already at Pav 10 when Frank and I arrived the next day. Leticia was busy inspecting the computerized mechanism for operating the crane. I immediately began inspecting it too, as if the encounter there concerned a faulty crane mechanism. After all, Bob was probably wondering what we were all doing at Pav 10. I logged in and noticed that Bunker 8 still had room for at least 3 more containers. After we all went in, Frank and Leticia hauled part of the cargo to bunker 8 while Maggie and I went to Bunker 1. I motioned for her to disconnect her monitor while I disconnected mine. I rapidly unsealed the bunker and took her to the last container which I opened up for her to see. She almost fell back. I pulled her to the entryway and indicated she should reconnect her nub while she went to give Frank a hand and sent Leticia to join me.

When Leticia came over, I went through the same procedure: disconnected com-monitors and took her inside. Even through the suit you could tell that she was stunned. She grabbed my arm and looked again before she stepped back and went out. She was having trouble breathing but fortunately Frank and Maggie were there waiting for us. After closing the container again, I too stepped out and began sealing the bunker; afterwards, I rapidly reconnected my monitor.

That night the four of us met again and decided to have all of Team 4 meet at some point when Bob was ordered to go to the Lab and couldn't be monitoring all of us at once.

— It's dangerous for only some of us to know about it.

— We all need to know; maybe we could plan some strategy.

— The implications are horrible. No one returns. They bring us with the promises of good pay and our return in four years; they even offer to extend your Moon tour. That's what Peter did. He was on his second tour. That's how he had saved enough to make a down payment on a place back home.

— But when he decided to go home, after his second tour, he ended up like the others. No one makes it back.

— That means something happened when they arrived at the Lab and transport center before they left. I can't understand it.

— I can. Face it; it's a one way trip, folks.

— What's happening is clear. The shuttles that join the space ships in orbit are being sent up with minerals but not with returning Tecos. They don't want to use valuable shuttle or cargo space to transport us braceros back when they can take back more titanium or bauxite in their payloads.

— But is this happening to all the workers or only to some. After all, we are the fourth expedition here. We know what happened to the third. What happened to the other two?

— Wasn't there a member from the first team that we met at the training site before coming here?

— But was he really from that first team or was it somebody who said that he had been up here. With the monitors they are able to see everything that we see up here and can talk about it as if they had seen it themselves.

— You mean, nobody has made it back down?

— It's a possibility.

— Hell, do you think they're really paying our salaries as they say?

— Shit, they better be paying. I'll contact my family and see if they have received any of the transfers through the bank.

— You think anyone here is also involved?

— It could only be Bob. He's the only one who was here before we arrived.

— We'll have to wait for Bob to go to the Lab for one of his monthly meetings before we can let the others know.

But first, the four of us would need to look for all the sensors at the base. For that I needed to assemble a monitor of our own that could tap into the monitors in Bob's office. Although he spent a good part of his time before the monitors, he was also in charge of bringing over the supplies from the warehouse facility near the Lab. If the mining complex was unable to send someone after their rations, Bob would bring their supplies to our station and let them know that they should send someone after them. Once last month he had even taken the supplies over himself as the miners had been behind schedule and needed to meet their production quota. That should have told us something right there.

· · · · · · · · · · · ·

In the meantime things continued as usual. During one day shift Frank and I were riding our jeeps out toward Pavilion 10 when we saw him.

— Look! Look!
— What is it, Frank? What is it?
— It's Peter. Stop. Stop.

I stopped the jeep and Frank jumped out and began running toward a figure in the distance. I ran as fast as I could and grabbed him by the arm.

— Let me go, Lydia. Let me go. It's Peter.

We could both see him directly in front of us, but he was not in his spacesuit. He had on a t-shirt, jeans and sandals. It was incredible. Yes, we could both see him. I saw him too. It was a mirage.

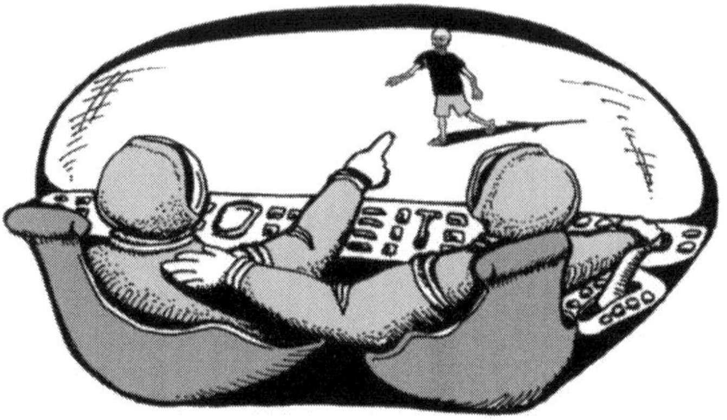

I quickly turned off my com system and pressed Frank's arm buttons as well. As soon as we turned off the com system, the mirage was gone.

— Someone's fucking with us, Frank. Someone's messing with our minds.

⟶ ⟩ ⟩ ⟩ ⟩ ⟩ ▸ ▸ ▸ ● ● ● ● ●

The day Bob went to the warehouse, I was able to make off with a discarded monitor that he had trashed in the disposal container outside his cubicle. I also made off with cells and cables from the supply unit in Bob's office. I had seen how the monitors operated once when he was having problems fixing some bugs in his newest monitor and he had asked for my help. It was a series CTO type that I had worked on in prison.

Tapping into Bob's own monitors was possible after a few months and we were able to find the various sensors set throughout the station. Of course I fully realized that there might be other hidden ones that were not connected to a monitor 24/7, except at unusual times, when I was out working and unable to check his screens, but we still had to take a chance.

The next time that Bob went to the lab for his meeting, we waited for 2 hours to ensure that he was far enough away and then I disabled all the monitors and sensors for 15 minutes. We all met at the dinner table while Frank explained as briefly as possible what we had discovered. We needed to know what had happened to the others, search for evidence related to the previous teams. Perhaps only the first team returned to Earth. Had any of the others returned? Were they also dead and buried in one of the containers. All I knew, as I told them, was that we needed to be very careful.

All hell broke out then at the table and everyone was talking at once. Betty, the other woman on the team, began screaming and the men pounded the table and swore to get to the bottom of things and if need be to strike back. The hardest thing was getting people to calm down as the 15 minutes off line came to an end. My last words were a warning. It was extremely dangerous to let on that we knew anything. If we gave the slightest indication that we knew or even suspected something, it would probably be sure death for everyone. It was especially important that Bob not suspect anything.

    Each team member went to his or her cubicle, except for Maggie, Leticia, Frank, and me who stayed at the table talking about music, as if nothing were wrong. Afterwards I went to Bob's office and re-connected all the monitors and sensors. Back in my cubicle later that day I again tapped into Bob's monitors to see if they were all back up and running. I checked on everybody on the monitor and found people awfully quiet in their cubicles, either covering their heads or doing what looked a lot like praying or something.

    The next shift we had the other three team members, Betty, Jake and Sam, schedule an inspection of Pavilion 10 so that they could see the container as well. Knowing about it was one thing but seeing it with their own eyes proved to be very difficult. The sight of bodies that had burst with bones sticking out was not something any of us would ever forget. We had to remind them to control themselves before turning their monitors back on. Bob might be away but they could see everything we saw back at the Lab, except for those few minutes that our nubs were off. But now everyone knew. We were all in it together and together we would have to find a way out. That night we all sat around in the dining room, listening to some music and drinking. It was all we could do. Jake began talking about things back home and Sam said his girlfriend would be waiting for him. Sure, Betty had snickered. We were starting to fall into a state of cynical depression and that was dangerous. It became clear that we had to do something to maintain some kind of hope alive.

〉〉〉〉〉〉▸▸●●●●●

Yes, our space suit was flexible. It had to be in order to allow us to move with some degree of ease. It had its own air conditioning, a liquid cooling system and its own oxygen supplier. The space helmet had a retractable visor for the sun and a defogger since the mask often fogged. We had access to a water pipette in case we became thirsty. From the inside of the helmet we could read an instrument panel indicating the temperature outside on the moon surface and inside the suit. The helmet also had small mirrors that enabled us to see behind and off to the sides while facing forward. Our sleeves had a series of small panels with bio readings we were supposed to check every so often. We also had com-monitors that allowed us to use our implanted transmitters to communicate with each other and with Bob back at the base. Everything we saw through the helmet was captured on a screen back at the base as well. Fortunately these AV monitors could be turned off momentarily. Back in the 21st century the suits used to be quite heavy; some weighed up to 183 lbs on earth, but the newest ones only weighed about 20 lbs on the moon; still they were bulky and not the easiest thing to move about in.

    We all had an emergency oxygen supply in case of an emergency. In theory, we could wear the suits for up to 7 or 8 hours before returning to the base to replenish the oxygen supply, no matter what the temperature was, but in practice it had been discovered that with the rise in temperature, the temp control system would tend to overload and limit the number of hours that we could be out on the surface. That is why we tended to work only 4 hours at a time, 5 max and to take breaks of about two hours before going out again. When the temperature rose above 180 degrees F, we stayed at the base and made sure all the gear, tools, oxygen tanks, com system and jeeps were in working order. If absolutely necessary we went out for no more than an hour. What had been learned already back in the 20th century was that if an astronaut became excited or hyperventilated for any reason, a condition measured in British Thermal Units, he would consume much more oxygen. Jeeps now allowed greater travel distances but we never wanted to find ourselves low on oxygen, far from base, or worse, lost and unable to return.

That's why the group always worked in the same area. That way we could look out for each other in case of a malfunction or an emergency.

⟩⟩⟩⟩⟩▸▸●●●●

— Yeah, Lydia's version is minimalist; she gives you a bird's eye view of things, and in the process makes things sound all right when in fact there was a lot that was really quite gross, grotesque and hazardous. The long days we could tolerate more or less, but the 14 day nights drove us up the wall. I often thought we'd all go insane, and we got on each other's case about the least little thing. We snarled and snapped at each other and sometimes fights broke out. The food was insipid and I began to think that I would not be able to stand 4 years out in that desolate moonscape. The beer tasted like urine, even ice cold, and the water was gross; only the nuts seemed to arrive in good shape, that is, unless they accidentally were exposed to air if the wrapping tore, making them all soggy and sour. The spacesuit we had to wear chafed our skin and made it difficult to maneuver when operating the cranes and bulldozers. The so-called high tech often failed and Lydia and Frank had to try mending what was sloppily put together back on Earth. I wasn't the only one that spent many hours all drugged out to try to cope with the unending nighttime. But it was when we learned that the Space Center had scheduled a little flight plan change at the end of our Moon tour, that we all woke up; it then became extremely important to live and that's when we developed solidarity and became like a family. Por eso, chico, soy tu tío, tu negro Sam.

⟩⟩⟩⟩⟩▸▸●●●●

So began our slow under-the-radar inspection of the other pavilions. We double checked all the delivery logs noting carefully whether the bunkers indicated full or almost full containers. Whenever a container appeared to be closed incompletely, Frank and I would go check it out. In two months we discovered two other containers with human remains. One thing was clear. Because only the communication technicians like me and Frank had the codes and knew how to seal and unseal containers, whoever was closing the containers knew a bit about the sealing protocol but was unable to do it effectively. But only up close inspection would reveal that a container was not properly sealed. Someone who was trying to finish his or her task ASAP and get back to the base would not pay particular attention to containers marked as sealed on the local computer. No one wanted to add to anyone's work load or hassle your own teammates.

Only one other person in the area knew enough about sealing the containers to input the wrong information and fool the monitor or the computer—and that was Bob. But even Bob did not have the code or skill to seal them properly or to recode the program. Only Frank and I knew how to do that. I then created a coded locking program on the sealing and unsealing of containers so that only Frank and I, who knew the new code, could set it. I remember thinking at the time that by the time they uncovered the new subprogram we would probably be dead too.

When Bob returned from the Lab and warehouse facility, I found him unusually pleasant; he brought goodies for everyone: cookies, peanuts and sunflower seeds, as well as the dehydrated food packages and dried fruits and vegetables that had just arrived. He sounded very happy, full of jokes, but we all met him with less than spirited faces.

— What's up? What's going on here? Did someone just die?

— Must be that we're getting close to the one-year blues, Betty replied.

— What you all need is a bit of Bourbon that I just happen to have here.

— What I'd like to do is send a message home.

— Sure, Lydia. Just come by in the morning and I'll connect you with the lab relay station.

— Where are Jake and Sam?

— They're already asleep. It was a tough day for them at the new site.
    — Well, I think I'll close up shop myself. It's been a long day for me too.
    The next day I sent the following message home.
    — Hi, Dad. Hope everyone is well there. We're all fine up here. How is the cócono? Ready to be roasted? Let me know. — Lydia. My father and I had agreed that "el cócono" or turkey would be code for our transfund account, where my pay was to go. When it was "ready for roasting," they would have enough to pay off some debts. When he said that it had been roasted and eaten, I would know that they had enough to leave the Reservation.

　　　　　　　))))))))●●●●●

— Tell me again, Momma, about how Dad saw Uncle Peter. You saw him too, didn't you?
    — Yes, we both saw him, but your father saw him first. You had to be looking straight ahead toward the horizon, but I was driving the jeep and focusing on the vehicle's fuel gauge at that moment.
    — Perhaps it was Uncle's ghost.
    — Who have you been talking to? No, m'hijo, unfortunately there are no ghosts; we are only matter, material stuff that decays, dust to dust, as they say. No, this was something else. It was Bob's way of getting his jollies by frightening us or shocking us. Of course he had no idea that we knew what had happened to Peter, but he wanted us to think that despite Peter's return to Earth, some part of him had remained on the Moon and it could reappear to those that related to him. Or perhaps in his own twisted way he was letting us know that Peter was dead on the Moon. In any case, the sighting was sure to become a topic of conversation back at the base. He expected us to get all shocked and frightened; perhaps something similar would happen to us. What really got to me was my failure to suspect anything beforehand. I

should have known better than to trust the communicator system; even so, something told me at that moment that we had to turn it off.

— How did he work it, Momma?

— You see, we had all thought that the communicator only functioned to let the Lab or Bob see everything that we were seeing. It also indicated the precise spot where we were standing or driving or digging or working. In case of any danger or mishap it would be possible to find us in short order. What I should have known is that virtual images or holograms could be telecast to us through the communicator as well. As soon as Frank started screaming and running out of the jeep to meet Peter, I ran out after him as well. I could see Peter directly in front of us, about 100 meters away. The image of Peter never got any closer nor did he seem to see us. I knew then that I had to turn off Frank's communicator and mine as well. I pressed his sleeve button and then mine. Like I told you before, we were able to do that for seconds and even up to 2 minutes, for personal hygiene and such. When we saw the image disappear we knew we had been duped and we both felt embarrassed to think we had fallen for it. Frank was so angry when he realized what had happened and that he had fallen for a virtual image that I immediately worried that he would return to the base and beat the shit out of Bob. I had to calm him down and remind him of our situation before reconnecting our nubs.

— What did you two do when you got back to the base?

— We said nothing about it, but later after dinner, Frank told Bob he wanted to send a message to his brother back on Earth. That allowed Bob to think that we had fallen for it. Two days later we received a response from Peter saying he was fine and busy but hoped to be able to write more soon.

— You knew he was dead by then?

— Oh, yes, by then we knew. That's what made it all the more infuriating. Clearly Bob was not the only one involved. They had to know about the deaths of the techs at the Lab and Communication Center as well as back home at the Terrabase. They were all in on it. Bob and the Lab as well were playing with our minds. That is a form of torture. I knew then that we would get back at them, at Bob and Lab Director, one way or another.

〉〉〉〉〉〉♦♦●●●●●

During the next three months two additional containers that were not quite full were discovered. Jake, Betty, Sam, Maggie and Leticia had become quite observant and were able to detect minute evidence. They had stopped carrying out their tasks mechanically, like before, and were now doing it with a great deal of care. We continued to have our off-line meetings whenever Bob left the station. The day we drank to our second year as Moon Tecos we all became depressed by the thought that what it really meant was that our time was running out. We only had two more years left, before we too could end up containerized.

At one of our meetings Jake suggested that there was a distinct possibility that what had happened to the waste management techs might be happening to the miners as well. Why not, he said, it sure would make both operations more "cost effective," right? That suggestion was met with both shock and words of solidarity. If the same thing was happening to all of us, there might be hope for us too. We decided to speak to Jeb or Tom from the mining camp, the next time one of them came after supplies. Jake knew Jeb from before. They were both from the Sacramento area and had played ball together. Frank knew Tom; both were from Calexico. So, we decided to somehow arrange a meeting with each one of them separately.

Another month passed before Bob scheduled a shipment of supplies for the mining crews. It was Jeb who came to pick them up. Frank and I were out in our jeep, playing a real oldie that we both could hear through our helmets: "Midnight Train to Georgia." We were both humming and singing along: "I'd rather live in his world than live without him in my world is his..." I still hadn't learned all the words but for some reason I loved that song. So damn syrupy and all. We sped up in order to intercept Jeb in his transport before he headed back to the mining camp which was about sixty miles away. It took a while before we were able to convey through hand signals the message: he needed to turn off his monitor for a few minutes. Using caló and ASL, both of which Jeb understood a bit of, Frank was able to communicate what we had discovered. What we wondered was whether any of the mining team members had made it back alive. Jeb's was only the third mining team on the Moon. Unlike the Tecos, the miners were signing up for six year stints. Jeb was now in his fifth year. Unbelieving at first, he said he would try to find out about previous mining teams, but that he thought we must be mistaken.

〇 ） ） ） ） ） ▶ ▶ ▶ ● ● ● ●

— No, Lydia, I don't see now how we're going to be able to leave this Reservation. All of our relatives are broke and most of them are on a Reservation, here, in Modesto, or in Sacramento. Who are we going to get to sponsor us to get out of here? Besides, we're in debt up to our necks, considering the debt we came in with and what it's grown since then. The clothes and other stuff that we get come out to more than our allotted stipend. Some of that becomes part of our debt. How are we going to pay off our debt, m'hija. I get no salary for my work here, and there are 5 of us now. I just can't see it.

— The day that Ricardo and I graduate and find jobs, Apá, we'll pay off your debt, our debt. You'll leave the Reservation one of these days. I swear it. You'll see.

〇 ） ） ） ） ） ▶ ▶ ▶ ● ● ● ●

But of course, I never did graduate and get a job to sponsor us out of there; instead I ended up in prison and then on the Moon. My brother Ricardo wasn't going to be able to do it on his own, either. That's also why I decided to take the Moon offer; it got me out of that prison and it would help my family, so I thought.

⟨⟩⟩⟩⟩▸▸◆◆●●●

Alguna vez tenías que saberlo, Pedro, cómo fue que murió tu padre biológico, Gabriel. Yes, I know he's unreal to you. Your real father is Frank, but someday you may want to know and you can look back on what I'm writing you. I've tried to put down some of our lessons and conversations, but there are other things that you may wonder about later, when we're gone and up North, Frank and me and your aunts and uncles; there might not be anyone around to answer your questions about more personal and political issues. Of course, Tom and Betty will be able to answer questions about the Moon and everything that happened subsequently, although we've talked about that a lot already, and you'll also have our notes, comments and conversations on your nano-text.

    Gabriel, as I told you, was in Brazil when he discovered what the bio-technical corporation was up to. At first he did not know that this corporation was part of a military complex experimenting with natural resources, both plants and humans. One of the labtechs managed to get away, and sent me an encrypted message from Gabriel with a few notations of his own added at the end.

    Gabriel was caught conferring with three indigenous leaders; this was after he had managed to get word to them about the need for an urgent meeting. They met at a designated spot, wellhidden, they thought, from outsiders. The leaders had their support hidden nearby and would surely have been killed if the tribesmen had not descended upon the group of soldiers that had apparently been following Gabriel and two other assistants and attempted to take them all prisoners. To avoid an all out battle with the tribesmen, and after several soldiers had been killed, the soldiers backed off but only after taking Gabriel and two others back with them. Many years later, when we were already here in Chinganaza, I was able to contact the tribe and one of the chieftains told me about the encounter and about their subsequent refusal to participate in the experiments run by the bio-tech company that was supposed to provide health assistance to the communities. When they realized the type of experiments that were being conducted, they retrieved their people, those that had survived the experiments anyhow. Once they returned to their villages with horror stories, the tribes prepared to attack the laboratory, despite their awareness of the sophisticated biological weapons that were stored at the lab. Rather than annihilate the entire area, a genocide that would have been impossible to hide, the pharma decided to move the lab into a new community further north, towards the Venezuelan border.

Gabriel and the other two, on the other hand, were taken to a prison inside the lab walls where they were tortured. The security people working at the lab wanted to know how much they knew and how much they had passed on to the chieftains. I already knew that he had been killed from the message I received from one of the lab techs that managed to leave, but what I didn't know then was that Gabriel had been tortured, water-boarded, electrocuted, made to stand for hours and sodomized with sticks. At first he refused to say anything but later he told them what he knew, what he had told the chiefs, but the soldiers thought he knew more, about the experiments being practiced on the natives, about the various animal to human transplants and vice versa. But all Gabriel knew about were the organ removals for sale to save the lives of high paying customers and political leaders. When they couldn't get more information out of him, they executed him.

The tribes only found out about the other transplant experiments when they were able to retrieve a number of "patients" who were later examined by other doctors; in fact these were Chinese doctors interested in knowing what was going on in the jungles of the Amazon. All of the human guinea pigs died soon thereafter.

  The message from the lab tech that I received was apologetic. "Lydia, there was nothing that I could do. When I wheeled him out of his cell, a day before he was executed, he was already una piltrafa humana, but he could still remember. He begged me to send word to you and told me where he had hidden the nano-cell. I told him that if I ever managed to escape that you would receive it. I'm sending this message to your friend Cecilia. She'll send word that Gabriel has been executed; the day you leave prison you'll be able to hear the rest of it. Good-bye, Lydia."

  I actually received word of Gabriel's death while I was still in prison, not knowing how word had gotten through; it was only when I left to join the Moon project that Cecilia brought me the nano-cell, which I know by heart. I asked Cecilia to keep it for me. I hope to see her again and if she still has it I will send it to you through friends. If not, you'll still know the gist of what happened and why it is important that these pharma companies not be allowed to come into our village not ever, nunca jamás.

  And that, son, is how you and I both lost your father. How could Gabriel have been your father, you say. I know it's sort of complicated. Okay, you know full well about the cryonics technology that's available today just about all over the place. One can freeze almost any kind of human tissue, sperm, eggs and fertilized eggs. That's what we did one summer that we went to a conference in Mexico as part of a research group from the university. We had fertilized eggs frozen and preserved in a cryonics lab. We had to pay a certain amount yearly and after we went to prison my brother Ricardo kept up the payments, just in case I ended up dead. By then he had a job and was able to continue paying when I went to the Moon. For our part, back then, Gabriel and I had begun to suspect that there was a spy in our political group and we began to think we might end up disappeared. We had no plans to marry but we did plan to spend the rest of our lives together. Anyhow, if one of us died and the other lived, there was still the possibility of our having a child together. The truth is you almost didn't make it, Pedro.

⟨ ⟩ ⟩ ⟩ ⟩ ▶ ▶ ● ● ● ● ●

Six weeks later Jeb returned to our station again on a supply run for the mining camp, but did not go directly to the base, as was standard procedure. Instead he traveled to the site of construction of the new pavilion. There he met Jake and Sam at the site.
    — Hey, Jeb, whassup?
    — Jake, bro, you guys inviting me to the base or what? I need to talk to Frank and I need a drink.
    They contacted us, we made up some excuse about needing to check out something at the new construction site and rode out to meet them. Jeb said they needed our help out at the mining camp with one of the computerized excavators. We scheduled a trip to the mining site the next day and agreed to take Jeb back to the base camp with us and ride out together the following day. Before leaving the site, we disconnected our monitors and during those few miles, Jeb told us that one of the miners knew a member of the former team and had tried to reach him on Earth but couldn't contact him. He'd disappeared. Jeb had not yet said anything to the other miners, except for Tom. Both now felt it important for us to go speak to the mining team. They needed to know.
    We told Jeb that all the team members had seen the remains, except for Bob, of course, whom we all had come to suspect had more than a little to do with what had happened to the others. Bob, of course, would be at the base to receive Jeb when we arrived. Later, Bob said he was surprised that Jeb had come all the way out here when he could have requested the assistance through the com system, but added that he figured that Jeb might have ulterior motives and that Betty was the real reason for his visit. In fact Jeb made it a point to sit with her and Jake, confirming Bob's suspicions. Better that than have him think anything else was going on.

It took several hours by jeep to arrive at the Exochev mining camp, as dust storms made it difficult to advance without stopping. We knew that Bob would report our absence, explaining that they'd requested technical and geological assistance there. We were supposed to be available and provide technical assistance to the various teams working on the Moon, although up to that time we had worked exclusively in the Cone Crater area and primarily with the waste management disposal unit at the base. The miners were an important aspect of the lunar colonization project; if anything, their work was more arduous than ours. Since the discovery of certain iron ores and bauxite, they had been given monthly quotas to fill. These minerals were then transported to the Lab for various experiments and then they were loaded in containers for shipment back to Earth.

After arriving at the mining station we met the Exochev miners and had dinner with them. Although there were many more miners at other various sites, there were some thirty miners at this particular station. All had arrived at the same time, almost five years before. On the second day (Yes, yes, I know. I keep saying "day" as if it were an Earth day, but the truth is we divided the hours as if we were on Earth, even though on the moon it was still the same day. Quit correcting me smarty pants, Pedro, or I'll start calling you Pedrito again.) we went out to the mines supposedly to assess the efficiency of their equipment. Tom led us deep into one mine where the entire team came together to inspect the equipment. Tom signaled for quiet. Our monitors were immediately turned off like those of everyone else there; being down so deep the com-monitors often went out so no suspicions would be aroused. Just in case we talked to them in a mixture of Spanish and ASL. At first they really didn't see what we were getting at when we said that we had a problem, a very serious problem. Tom explained that the problem might not just be ours but theirs as well. None of them could confirm for sure that the previous miners had made it back to Earth. When that sank in, the men were stunned and they wanted to get an explanation from someone. Some threatened to go out right then and there; one man insisted on going immediately back to the Lab station and asking to be returned to Earth on the next ship.

It took a while for Tom and Jeb to calm the Exochev men down. First of all we had no real proof that the previous mining teams had never made it back. Second, if they had been disappeared, it was important to find evidence, perhaps at the old mining sites, at the first pits that had been used before tunneling gave better results. Moreover, if their elimination was in the works, they at least had time, a year at least, before their contract was up and by then they could come up with a way to defend themselves.

Ultimately we hoped the miners would join forces with the Tecos and together we could resist and somehow at least guarantee our return to Earth when our contracts were up. It was important to begin spreading the word and organizing. Perhaps the miners needed to contact the Chinese workers that were operating mines on the other side of the Moon or even the workers at the European mines, mostly African miners. Isolation was working against us and there was a lot to be done.

We talked about an hour and left later that day after agreeing to stay in touch. One of the things we had been able to do during our meeting was develop a code for communicating with each other. The fact that Tom and Frank knew each other from before came in handy and also averted suspicion somewhat.

When we got back to the base I had a transmission from home:

— "Hija, acá todo bien. Your mother and Lupita send their hugs and kisses. As for the cócono, not a feather in the corral. He probably flew away. Take care. - Your Dad."

I immediately circulated the message and that night after Bob went to his cubicle, we spoke briefly about the news. The idea that our salaries were not being deposited, as I now knew mine were not, made us even angrier and distrustful. It was important that each of us verify whether this was the case or not, by transfund accounts and sending messages to family and friends. Perhaps my prison record kept mine from being transferred, like Maggie suggested, or, perhaps, none of us were getting paid and never would be.

〉〉〉〉〉●●●●●●●

Running against the wind. Yes, that's the song I sometimes hum or sing. Well, yes, it's a metaphorical expression. It's this sense that one is always running up against the odds, against obstacles, against the norm, against the wind, in opposition. One can run with the wind too, but that means going along, conforming. But it's not always possible since we're not all sheep that just follow along; sometimes we take off in a different direction, contrary to what's expected of us. We have the option to choose, at least sometimes, if we're lucky. That's what some call agency, Pedro. It's a way of saying that we're not totally programmed, although in part we're all brainwashed. But even to know that is to fight it. You can't choose a lot of things, not your blood circulation or your breathing patterns, or your digestion, or even your skin color, but at a social level, Pedrín, we can sometimes, not always, make choices. Some species have few choices. See that butterfly. It's coming out of its cocoon; almost looks like plastic, right? Wasn't it a few weeks ago that we saw the larva eating away at the leaves. And now here it is, a beautiful orange butterfly with black wing tips. It's a beautiful Monarch. From here it will leave and make its way out there in the world, frankly without too many options. It will try to fake that it is a leaf when it rests on a tree, but it'll probably end up as a meal for a bird or a lizard, or even trapped in a spider web. Yeah, you're right, the butterfly too will end up flying against the wind. It's just that we tend to be too anthropocentric and think that we are the center of the universe, when of course we are not, never have been, never will be.

〉〉〉〉〉●●●●●●●

Unlike our site where we had containers that we could check out, at the mines there were only pits and tunnels. The miners, as Tom and Jeb reported, had begun by inspecting the previous mine sites but they found nothing suspicious, only sandy piles, basalts and other rocks everywhere.

— This is the last excavation the previous miners made, Tom.

— Yeah, sort of interesting that with each new team, a new mining site gets designated for us to carve up.

— We should turn over some of these rocks, maybe. Bring over the robotic crane, Jeb.

— Nothing here, Bill. Let's try further up the tunnel, at the place where they said they found a rich titanium deposit.

There they again found piles of rocks everywhere, but the piles here seemed to be in some type of order, not at random. One of the piles was higher than the others and rather than digging up the wall, it appeared that the digging had been in an area below the pile of rocks.

— Jeb, move that crane down over here.

— I told you there's nothing but rocks here. There's nothing to find.

— Okay, okay

— Hey, Tom, perhaps we also need to dig down into this hole a bit.

— O.K., Bill, get the robotic excavator. It'll go faster that way. After removing the rocks with the crane they began digging and the sand began to fall too easily, as if the ground were not compact. After a few minutes of digging they hit something solid that wasn't a rock.

— Over here, Jeb. Shovel it out a bit. More. Easy…

They saw the arms and legs first. All three froze for a second. They had all been hoping that they wouldn't find anything. Instead of continuing the dig, Tom decided to cover the hole and return the rocks to where they had previously been piled.

— Just in case they might come checking around; we don't want them to know that we know.

The next day Frank got a message from Tom: "Nos fileriaron, cabrón." With that we knew what their search at the old mine pits had produced; the macabre findings confirmed what we had all feared. We started thinking about extending our search ourselves; perhaps we should search the earlier pavilions, the ones that had been excavated when Team 2 arrived.

What to do next was the big question. Who else could they contact for support? Should we try to see if any research workers at the Lab were involved, or were there previous lab team members unaccounted for too? Should we contact the pilots that flew the shuttles? Were the Lab directors in on it? Were they in fact the ones who had ordered the disappearance of the workers or were orders coming directly from Earth? Should we even try to contact the Chinese colonists or some of the European workers at other mining sites? We did not know. But at least now the group in the know included the thirty Exochev miners and the seven Tecos at Cone Crater.

))))))))))))

Yes, Sam's right, Pedro. Our meals up there were pretty insipid; dehydrated meals can't be anything but gross and that's despite the fact that I took along a good bit of dried chile peppers or what we here call ají. The only good part, I guess, was that we had beer, wine and other alcoholic drinks. Every so often a shipment of munchies arrived and we enjoyed our nuts and peanuts. We took vitamin supplements everyday. How many times can you have the same dried piece of meat? It all tasted the same anyhow. Right, like chicken. yeah, the cubicles were very small. The entire base station was small; rather claustrophobic, actually; But to tell you the truth, perhaps because I came from the Reservation and had spent time in a prison cell I could deal with the close quarters. The sense of imprisonment is something that you can get used to, I think. Do you realize what I just said? It's horrible, as if one were a guinea pig or a lab rat. And come to think of it, all of that was normal, somehow natural. The thing is that only participation in collective action ever gave me a sense of freedom, a sense of being more than a caged animal, whether on the Reservation, in prison, or up on the Moon for almost two years.

◦))))) ▶ ▶ ● ● ● ● ● ●

We figured that the pilots had to be in on it; otherwise they would have said something about flying the shuttles back to the orbiting ship without any crew members aboard. The astronauts on board the ships coming from Earth had to know too since they kept bringing supplies for mining, waste and lab teams that continued to be relatively small. If the other crew members had remained on the bases, the food supplies would have needed by this time to be tripled, at least. The nauts were rotated, that was true, but we were convinced that they had to know what was going on, just as did the shuttle pilots that rendezvoused with the ships and returned with supplies.

With the Lab people, it was another story; they had not changed. Except for the director, who had been to Earth a couple of times, all the other researchers had been at the Lab since it was started up in 2110. In addition to the director, there were three couples working at the lab, among them a pair of astrophysicists from Canada, supervising four assistants, some working on particular projects dealing with solar storms and the discovery of new galaxies and planets, all using the Moon's vantage point to conduct research and experiments to prove or disprove a variety of theories, dealing with "branes" and the so-called "String Theory." Some were carrying out experiments with promising lunar minerals, but the Director also was in charge of shipping particularly profitable minerals back to earth. These astro-physicists planned to spend at least 20 to 30 years on the Moon before returning to Earth. They were also training the astro-physicists of the future; each one had a chair at a prestigious university. Some had already published major papers on their findings. They stayed in their own lab compound and really had nothing much to do with the rest of us lowly techs, whether miners or waste disposal techs, nor wanted to. Cynically, we agreed that their transfunds were probably being processed just fine.

We discussed all of this one afternoon when Bob went to the Lab. It was decided not to trust anyone from the compound, not the Lab assistants nor the physicists. The small security contingent stationed at the Lab, it turned out, was there to protect the Director and the other scientists, not to police the work sites. Whatever was going on at the Lab was considered high-value, worthy of safeguarding.

— Don't you think, Frank, that there appears to be a hierarchy up here, with the Lab Directors on top having the power over life and death and we the grunts, with no say-so in any matter, on the bottom?

— No shit. Like everywhere, Lydia. Why should it be different here?

Our "discovery" had hit Frank hard.

— Because it's a relatively new space where new forms of relating can develop. And yet we find the same power structure here. Recapitulation. Who was it that said, "Déjà vu all over again"?

— Yeah, right. Always the idealist. Look around. If they killed and freeze-dried Team 3, you can imagine what they did to the first two. We just haven't found them yet. We're expendable and not worth the cost of transport back to Earth once our replacements appear. That's what, 7 Tecos at an average 60 kilos a piece? Why that's almost 500 kilos of titanium they could ship back instead, Frank added sarcastically and then went quiet.

〉〉〉〉〉♦♦♦●●●

— Momma, did you dream on the Moon?

— Yes, I had some rather spectacular dreams, but not at first since I was waking up every hour or so. Later when we had settled in and established a routine, then I had some interesting dreams, but nothing to write home about.

Maggie was the one with the dreams or nightmares in our group. Everyday during breakfast she'd tell us about her dreams, some were just silly, others, nightmares. I was always into narrative and eager to hear something different as the video cells, even the bootlegged ones, were often viewed eight or ten times, till we practically had all the parts memorized. Maggie's dreams, on the other hand, were always different. The three that I remember best were all nightmares.

After we discovered the bodies in the container, Maggie had a weird dream.

— What did you dream last night, Maggie. You look a bit desvelada, like you didn't sleep well.

— I had a horrible dream last night.

— Well, let's hear it.

— We were all on a shuttle heading toward the orbiting space station. Sam was at the controls and Jake was assisting him. We were all sitting back in our seats, still in our spacesuits, when suddenly the shuttle started shaking all over.

— What's happening? We all screamed.

— I'm feeling pulled into some gravitational zone.

— That's impossible, Sam.

— Hang on. Oh, m'god. I can't believe it. Look up ahead, Jake.

— Good God!

— What? What? I screamed and ran up to the cockpit. There before my eyes was a black nothingness that was pulling us into its core. All around I could see wisps of light. Our shuttle could not resist the attraction and all of a sudden we found ourselves falling into the vortex of a black hole.

I was still screaming when Leticia woke me up.

— I tell you! That's the last time I tell you all about black holes.

)))))))))•••••

To Bob's surprise. we began checking out the original pavilions,

— Why are you guys going back to those sealed pavilions? There's nothing there to check out.

— Just checking, Bob. We want to make sure that after five to ten years, everything is exactly as it's supposed to be. No shifting of containers, no problems with the seals, better safe than sorry, right? Besides, till Jake and Sam finish the new excavations, we won't be able to set up the bunkers or finish up the installations for Pavilions 13 and 14. Better than staying in here and picking our noses, right?

It was there that we found the bodies of Team 1 and Team 2. We wanted to place all the containers together, but that was going to be difficult unless we did it when Bob left the base. Luckily, we could count on his monthly trips to the lab for supplies. We made note of where the containers were and waited to place them all in Pavilion 10, with Peter, as soon as the chance presented itself, that is, as soon as Bob was away.

)))))))))•••••

The butterflies of Cali-Texas are different. We have the Monarchs there as well; but unlike up north, these Ecuadorian Monarchs migrate south from Mexico. How are they different? I'll tell you one thing. I think the butterflies of the Amazon region are more beautiful and there certainly is a greater variety. Do you see them? Yes, they're everywhere. There's one in your hair right now. The sad thing is that this area of the Amazon is the only one that has survived as jungle and as communal property, and that's thanks to the indigenous movements of the 21st century. You've heard the story, right? After the hemispheric wars, the indigenous coalitions of Ecuador's oriente gained ecological control of these lands and that's why once again it was possible to say, "El Ecuador es, ha sido y será un país amazónico." Because back in the 20th century, in 1942 the Rio de Janeiro protocol gave Peru all this Amazonian area. At that point the important thing for the U.S. was the second world war. Right? Right, yes, the Indigenous War of 2070 was the major war of the entire Andean region against the dispossession and exploitation of the remaining indigenous peoples. They had been inspired by the Zapatista Movement in Chiapas many years before. With this reterritorialization, limited as it was, the Indians regained some of their lands and managed to survive and flourish to a certain extent, although they are still today surrounded by NIO corporations that would love to get their hands on this area. But so far, so good. That's why we came here; you were born here; that's why we live here, Pedro.

·)))))▶▶■●●●●

When the ambient temperature rose to 200 degree F. no one even tried to go out, not even briefly. We began doing jobs at base camp. There was a lot to be done, especially with respect to the robotic instruments that we used. They tended to wear out because of the sand particles that got caught in the gears and relays. The space suits had to be checked for oxygen leaks; the com-monitors or nubs were all tested as were the audiovisual sensors. Besides, it was important to stay busy; less time to think about what had happened to Peter and all the others; otherwise we'd get depressed just thinking. No one was interested in returning to our programming lessons nor did we get into good discussions about space. Everyone was tense and we all feared that something was about to happen. The temperature had started to go down when it did. Bob came in one day when we were eating dinner.

  — What's happening here? Everyone seems to be weirding out.

  — Nothing, Bob, but, you know, we have a couple of questions to ask you.

  — Shoot. Did I forget to bring something back you wanted from the storehouse this last time I went?

— No, it's not about that. We want to ask you why you have sensors and monitors in all our cubicles. What? Are you running some kind of surveillance on us?

He was clearly surprised that we had found out. He couldn't hide it and he wasn't pleased.

— That's so that in case of an emergency, uh, I can communicate with each and every cubicle. In case one of you has an attack or something, you know, I have a way of finding out or hearing what's going on. All you need to do is say "help" and I'll be on my way to your cubicle, that's all.

— Know what, Bob, chinga tu madre. I just disconnected all the sensors and monitors in here. No one at the Lab Center can hear us or see us.

— What do you mean… What have you done, Lydia? I should have known it was you. Don't you know it's for our own safety. Go turn them back on. We need to be able to communicate with the Lab at all times.

— Exactly why I disengaged them, you hijo de la chingadísima.

— So, tell us, Bob. What do you know about the previous Tecos from Team 3 that were here before us?

— Well, nothing, except that they left. No one has sent me any messages from Earth, but then I wasn't expecting any since we didn't exactly become friends.

— You bastard.

Frank grabbed him by his shirt.

— You're going to tell us everything you know about the corpses in Pavilion 10, bunker 1 or I'll break your skinny pendejo neck.

Bob tried to break free but we all grabbed him.

— Tie him up, Maggie said, here use this.

— Fucker, either you tell us what you know or I'll break all your ribs, one by one.

— Jake, Jake, I don't know anything. I have no idea what you're talking about.

Jake punched him hard in the kidneys and then in the gut, repeatedly.

— All right, stop! What do you want to know? Stop!

— Who killed the seven men who are buried in the container?

—I don't know anything about that. I don't know nothing about where anybody's buried.

— Bullshit! Tell us what you know, hijo-de-la-chingada.

This time Sam hit him in the head hard.

— It's the supervisors, the supervisors, the Director, at the Lab. I had nothing to do with it, nothing at all. Really. They're the ones that decided to get rid of them to keep from having all that extra weight on the shuttles and ship.

— And how were they killed, cabrón?

— They were taken to the Transport Center, there near the Lab, where the landing runway is. They were supposed to leave from there, but before boarding they were invited to eat. That's how they were poisoned. They put it in the food and drink. That's how they died. One of the shuttle pilots told me. I wasn't there. I was already here with you guys.

— That's not what happened to my brother Peter, asshole, tell us the truth.

— Okay, Okay. Peter had already had a lot to drink before he left here. We had quite a party, if you remember. For that reason he did not have any of the food or drink at the transport station, but fell asleep at the table, like the others. But when they came to take them out to throw them on the rail flatbeds, he woke up and began to gag without his space suit. He began to convulse and then his eyes popped out of their sockets. That's when the pilot fired one shot into his temple. To put him out of his misery. Poor sonofabitch.

With that, Jake almost beat him to death. We stopped him and tried to calm him down. Frank, on the other hand, went cold, almost catatonic, to think of how his brother had died. When he finally came to, he also fell on Bob and began beating him mercilessly, not even aiming his blows.

— Dime, cabrón, has any one of the workers returned to Earth?

— No. Up to now, no…no.

— And what about the salaries? Are they really getting deposited in the Cali-Texas Bank?

— Some are, only for some. For the nauts, pilots, and astrophysicists at the Lab. For the last 3 months, nothing's been deposited in my account, and I know why. I know too much. I'm a liability. I have to be their accomplice and do whatever they say or I'll end up like your brother. I have to handle the surveillance and keep them informed of everything that goes on in the field and here at the base. I also keep tabs on the miners because we have monitors everywhere there as well.

— Who's the guy in charge at the mining camp? Who's "we"?

— I don't know.

— Who is it, desgraciado.

— It's a man named Ted, although lately he's been laying low. I think he's finally getting it and realizing that he too will be killed if he decides to return to Earth, once his contract runs out.

— So, what do we do with this fucking pinche buey now?

— You all know that I have to maintain daily contact with them or else they'll know that something's wrong.

—Your monitors are audio-visual, but do you communicate with them in the same way or by e-mail?

— I can send visuals for the "sensitive stuff," but mostly I send daily e-mails.

— Bob, I'll tell you what. In that case, your e-mails will arrive on time, as usual. Get off your ass and let's go on a visit to your control room right this minute.

A bit later that same day, five of us left in our jeeps while Maggie and Leticia stayed to watch prisoner Bob, bloody, bruised and tied up to his favorite chair. Leticia made sure Bob's reports were transmitted daily.

We proceeded to bring all the containers with bodies together. It took a good while because they were scattered in three different pavilions. We placed these containers on the rail flatbeds and took them all to Pavilion 10. We already had photos but we took some more. Before we left them there, we saw Frank mutter a few words before the container bearing his brother's body. We looked at each other, but no one said a word. There or on the way back. We then returned to the base. Between suiting up and moving the containers, it had taken us five hours to get the job done.

⋅ ⟩ ⟩ ⟩ ⟩ ▸ ▸ ● ● ● ● ●

I'M THE ONLY SURVIVOR OF THE PREVIOUS THREE GROUPS. WHEN THE OFFER WAS MADE FOR TRANSFER, I WAS THE ONLY ONE THAT ACCEPTED. FOR THAT REASON, I SURVIVED. I THOUGHT THEY WOULD SEND ME TO THE MINING CAMP, BUT THEN, AS IT WORKED OUT, I WAS NOT TRANSFERRED AT ALL. I WAS SIMPLY ASSIGNED TO SERVE AS THE COMMUNICATIONS TECH IN CHARGE OF SURVEILLANCE OF THE OTHER TECHS. MY JOB WAS REPORTING TO THE LAB ABOUT ALL THE ACTIVITIES OF MY PEERS. WHEN THE LAB SUSPECTED THAT I KNEW WHAT HAD HAPPENED TO MY TEAM, THEY MADE SURE OF MY CONTINUED COLLABORATION..
THEY MADE SURE THAT I WILL ALWAYS KEEP MY MOUTH SHUT AND THAT I WILL ALWAYS BE AT THEIR BECK AND CALL. I AM THEIR SPY AND AS TIME HAS PASSED I HAVE COME TO ENJOY MY POSITION AND THE POWER IT GIVES ME OVER THE NEWBIES, DESPITE MY KNOWING THAT I WILL NEVER LEAVE THIS PLACE.

⋅ ⟩ ⟩ ⟩ ⟩ ▸ ▸ ● ● ● ● ●

And that's what the prick we knew as Bob Cortés offered as an explanation.

⋅ ⟩ ⟩ ⟩ ⟩ ▸ ▸ ● ● ● ● ●

The idea that we were trapped on the Moon and that there were plans in place for us to never return home to Earth began to be unbearable. When nighttime came, that 14 day night seemed unending and the tension grew. We started picking fights with each other. The resentment and tension continued to rise and I feared that we would end up killing each other. I myself could not stand the wait, the uncertainty, the fear. I began to think I'd go crazy.

— Sam, if you play "Against the Wind" one more time, I'll kill you. And that's the truth.

— Look, lady, if you play "Midnight Train to Georgia," once more I'll break more than your cell player, Lydia.

— Calm down, everybody. Just calm down.

— Who died and named you king, Jake?

— I'll be damned. Me lleva la chingada con todos juntos. Don't you see what's happening?

At that moment Maggie walked in with a message from Tom at the mining camp. She looked at Leticia and knew something was up, but before turning around to get back to her prisoner Bob, she said:

— This just came for you, Frank, from Tom."

— Hey, Maggie, how did Tom manage to communicate directly with us?

— Those metallurgical engineers have it all figured out, hombre, and now that all-seeing Bob is out of commission, no hay pedo.

— Let's see. Let's see.

— "Greetings. Contacts made. Meeting scheduled. Send two or three. Early daylight hours best. Bring extra battery —direct route. No further contact. El Compa, Tom."

We had practically just been at each other's throats a minute ago and now everyone began talking at the same time, even sort of smiling, except Bob, who was still tied down in his chair in the control room. Maggie, who liked the jailer duties, only released him to go to the bathroom, under her very watchful guard, and to eat. Payback, she said, and we all understood.

Of course everyone wanted to be the one going to the meeting, but it was decided that since Frank and Jake knew Jeb and Tom well, it would be better if they went. It appeared from the "contacts made" reference that a Chinese representative would also be there and perhaps someone from the European Union camp. We decided to send Frank and Jake to the meeting with a proposal. We sat up all night working out the plan.

⁂

THE PRESUMPTUOUSNESS AND REBELLIOUSNESS OF THE TRASH TECHS! WHEN I TOLD THEM THAT THEY COULD NOT LEAVE THE MOON AND THAT WE COULD ONLY OFFER THEM THE OPPORTUNITY TO RE-ENLIST OR AWAIT TRANSFER TO ANOTHER COLONY, PREFERABLY A MINING COLONY —WE NOW HAVE SEVERAL ON THE MOON —THEY BEGAN TO SCREAM OBSCENITIES AT US, ESPECIALLY AT ME, AS HEAD OF THE LAB AND STATION. I TRIED TO EXPLAIN THAT WE NEEDED TO GET SOME ROCKS AND MINERALS TO EARTH AND THAT THEIR WEIGHT AS PASSENGERS WOULD PROHIBIT SHIPMENT OF MATERIALS NEEDED ON EARTH FOR THE DEVELOPMENT OF NEW WEAPONRY AND RESEARCH. IF OUR FINDINGS WERE CORRECT, IT WAS IMPERATIVE THAT CALITEXAS LAY CLAIM TO A HUGE AREA OF THE MOON BEFORE THE CHINESE AND EUROPEANS DISCOVERED WHAT WE HAD FOUND. THE TECHS WOULDN'T LISTEN AND BEGAN TO MAKE THREATS AGAINST US ALL. SOME OF THE LAB PEOPLE, ESPECIALLY THE STUDENT ASSISTANTS, WERE ALREADY TAKING THEIR PART. IT WAS THEN THAT I ACQUIESCED AND SAID THAT WE WOULD DELAY THE ROCK AND MINERAL SHIPMENT TO ENABLE THEM TO RETURN, BUT THAT THEY WOULD HAVE TO BEAR THE CONSEQUENCES ONCE IT WAS DISCOVERED ON EARTH THAT THEY WERE RESPONSIBLE FOR THE DELAY IN SHIPMENT.

I THEN GAVE ORDERS TO EMPTY THE SHUTTLES, UNLOADING THE CARGO THAT WE ORIGINALLY PLANNED TO SEND UP TO MEET THE SPACECRAFT, AND INVITED THEM ALL TO EAT, WHILE WE WAITED FOR THE UNLOADING. OF COURSE AS SOON AS THEY ALL STEPPED INTO THE MESSHALL, I RECALLED THE ORDER. CLEARLY IT WAS NECESSARY FOR THE FEW TO DIE FOR THE GOOD OF THE MANY.

No, you're right, it was not the first time that we had had to do this, but since two of them had already voluntarily re-signed up four years before, I thought that this time, the offer of steady work and the promise of a growing account back on Earth would lead to their collaboration, in hopes that at some future date it might be possible for us all to return. But no, these Techs that could at best look forward to menial jobs on a Reservation were unwilling to respond favorably to our offer. Of course we could have simply imprisoned them, but convict labor would require the installation of constraints and guards and I am not willing to redirect manpower nor are we ready to establish Reservations on the Moon. But that is coming, no doubt. For now, the important thing was to rid ourselves of a nuisance and did. I'll let you know how the new Techs work out. The presence of four women may further complicate things, although they are all highly skilled, especially the communications expert. Do let me know if our findings are corroborated at your research lab. I know it will take time. If so, there will be major changes up here in the near future. I'll contact you again in a few weeks. Over and out. Johnson.

))))))••••••

After discarding a number of ideas, we saw two feasible possibilities. 1) We would take control of the Lab compound and Transport Center without too much trouble and afterwards let Earth know what had been happening here. If they wanted operations to continue they would have to deal with us. But as Frank pointed out, the whole plan was probably hatched and run from the Houston Control Center and they would send us all to hell. Either we followed their orders or they would stop our shipments.

— They would stop sending all supplies, that's for sure, and we'd be screwed.

— Perhaps we could start cultivating gardens. We've been collecting our excrement and leftovers. You know, growing our own stuff hydroponically or whatever.

— Yeah, right, nice idea, Betty, but by the time that worked out, we would have starved. You know it'd take many months to set up.

— O.K. There'll be a new ship arriving on the 10th with supplies and to pick up a cargo. We'll have to make those supplies last for more than a month, to buy us time.

— We still have a good number of packages of dried fruit and meat.

— We'll need to take inventory and see how much we've got and for how many days. For sure we shouldn't do anything till after the 10th.

— We're okay for water, since it's extracted nearby.

— Yes, but we depend on the Lab for the supply of both water and oxygen, let's not forget that little detail, folks. They would have to be willing to continue to provide it for us. We already need to go there every two weeks for our water and oxygen.

— No, shit. I've been making that run ever since I came to this stinking rock. So, don't remind me.

— O.K., Sam, but unless we get our shit together, buy ourselves some time and manage to get ourselves off this stinking rock, back on Earth they'll just blame our deaths on some catastrophe and no one will know the difference.

— Right, but unfortunately they control all communications, all reports.

— We could take over the communication center. Lydia and Frank know how all that works, but I don't know if we've got the manpower.

— OK., so what's plan B. Let's hear it.

— OK. The second possibility is that we take over the Transport Center, next to the Lab compound, with all its communication systems and the shuttles and that we rendezvous with the ship that's arriving on the 10th and that we return to Earth on it and just get off this stinking rock.

— How many of us can fit in there. There are 7 of us here, 8 with Bob, and 30 at the Exochev camp. If others come on board, we may need several shuttles.

— There are, what?, 11 people at the lab , plus three pilots and 6 members of the security team. None of those people will want to leave with us, for sure.

— We can use the 3 shuttles to fly to the orbiting ship after they unload the supplies. They will expect the returning payload to be minerals; that space is for us.

— There are seats on the space craft for about 20 but without the regular payload we can probably all fit, that is, the miners and us Tecos.

— Hey, Frank, but what about Peter and the others? Are we going to just leave them here?

— Look, I know he's my brother, and I'm not cold or heartless or anything, but they're dead already. Let's get ourselves and the other live ones out of here first. There's only so much space and this, my friends, is in all likelihood a one-shot deal, no?

— What about workers at other mining camps?

— They depend on other Transport Centers and other shuttles, they'll need to do the same thing we're doing here, there, if they want to get out of this place.

— How many ships come to the moon?

— All told, there are 4 space ships that come in any given month, one to the Chinese colony, one to the European colony, one to this transport center and one to the BechtShell Mining Camp; that's the joint European- Cali-Texas venture.

— You got to know that at the first whiff of problems, they would send troops or a missile. Too much has been invested to risk losing it to the competition.

— That's for sure. They'll say that there is a lot of capital invested in these moon projects that needs to be protected and that our revolt is putting everything at risk. That's why it will be important to do everything on the quiet, without letting on what we are planning until we are ready, and there's no turning back.

— Hey, don't forget, we have to send Bob's daily message to the Lab. We don't want them to suspect anything. Everything is business as usual.

— But you know that when the ship arrives and Bob doesn't pick up the supplies, then they will know something is up.

— We could always say that he was indisposed, sick or something.

— By then, hopefully, it won't matter. When the next ship comes we will need to be ready to move on this, get all the details down.

— You know the devil's in the details.
— Yeah.

〉〉〉〉〉〉〉▶▶●●●●●

At night there, which, as I told you, lasts some 14 days, the sky looks just marvelous. From the moon you can see not only the Earth, but a sky full of millions of stars. There, like here, we would spend nights talking about the possibility of extraterrestrial life. The possibility of making contact with life forms from other planets, with intelligent beings, was something that each one of us fantasized about, some more than others. Hopefully these extraterrestrials were more intelligent than earthlings, anyhow. We always talked about how advanced they'd have to be in order to reach us. I would have loved to have worked at the Lab Observatory because astronomy and physics were always among my favorite subjects at the university, in addition to math and engineering, but without a doctorate, — I only did my first year of graduate work — there was no way that I could have been assigned to the Lab. But, "black holes" have always intrigued me, as well as the notion of the Big Bang. You know that there are those who think that our universe is headed for an implosion that will lead to the contraction of all matter so that it'll end up in a black hole again, ready to explode and initiate a new beginning. That's what happened before, when this universe was formed. Order out of chaos, as the Russian physicist Prigogine put it back in the 20th century. I think he got a Nobel Prize for that.

〉〉〉〉〉▶▶▶●●●●

— Bob, we haven't detected any inter-cellular communication from base monitors. Everything all right there?
— Everything's fine, Dr. Johnson. We're having a bit of difficulty with our inter-com system here at the base station, but a couple of the team members and I are working on it now. Should have it up and running in a few hours.
Maggie was making sure we stayed on top of things, but we also realized we had to be very careful.
— Shiiit! I knew it. They can even pick up what the damn sensors and monitors here at the base transmit. I thought only Bob could receive those messages.
— You better tell Leticia to run the detector again, in case we overlooked something.
— Come on, don't get paranoid on me, Sam. We can't overreact right now.
— Hey, Lydia, maybe we should turn on some of the monitors so that things appear normal, at least for a while. Let them get some normal feed from here. What do you think?
— Good idea, Maggie. Yeah, switch a few back on, just not the loading bay. O.K.?
Jake and Frank left at sunrise, which is much like twilight, taking an extra battery pack that allowed them to make the trip in their jeep without having to recharge it upon arrival at the mining camp, just in case. It would take 4 to 5 hours to get there. They took two extra tanks of oxygen as well, also just in case. Most importantly they took our second proposal, Plan B, the one we had all decided was more likely to produce a successful outcome, to the meeting. We had all agreed that an attempt at a return to Earth was the best option. The Lab people would be left behind but they would

be able to survive until the next ship arrived, as they would be well supplied; besides they weren't one of us.

The other colonies were also a concern, but we had to count on their organizing themselves to bring about change or their safe return. Today's meeting at the mining camp would clarify things. We knew about the Chinese colonies, the European colony and the inter-European-Cali-Texas mining camp, in addition to ours, but we did not know if other new colonies or projects had been initiated on the moon since we'd arrived. In fact, the population on the moon that we calculated in the hundreds had by then risen to over two thousand. We had been on the moon for almost two years and had heard little about what was happening back home. We now realized that only non-political messages from family members got through to us. Pretty much everything else was censored.

〉〉〉〉〉〉▶▶●●●●●

The Moon, the near side that we see from Earth, at least, is marked by huge extensions that astronauts call "smooth maria," as in the Oceanus Procellarum, that looks like a desert. But there are craters, canyons or rilles that cross the desert. On the far side or dark side of the Moon, the part that we cannot see from earth, there are no smooth plains; it is an area marked by the millions of meteorite blows that it receives and has received for thousands of years. I could never figure out how the Chinese had set up camps on the dark side. Perhaps they are closer to the near side than I thought. Over 4.6 billion years old, by now, the moon's near side appears to have mountains and in effect there are in the enormous craters volcanos that have spread their lava on the moon surface. Next to the mountains are gigantic rocks. Since the moon does not have a magnetic field, it receives the direct impact of solar storms; that's why the strong winds of nuclear particles would come down on us, penetrating the walls of the base and our space suits and helmets. As they hit our optic nerves we would see flashes of light.

When Frank and Jake returned from the mining camp, after the equivalent of four days, the first thing they told us about was the informer, that they, whoever they were, had implanted a receptor under the scalp of a miner, the miner named Ted. The reason he had been lying low was that the other miners had found out about him; that was even before Bill, Jeb and Tom announced the findings at the old abandoned mining pits. But a spy also might mean that the Lab already knew that we were investigating what had happened to the previous team members. For all we knew, Bob probably had a sensor in his scalp as well, one undetectable because of his long hair which he always wore in a ponytail. The miners had found that Ted's sensor lit up when something was wrong at the camp. Since they all wore special mining helmets the sensor had not been detected. Back at their camp, Ted always wore a baseball cap and he also had longish hair.

After hearing that, we all went to Bob's cubicle where we still had him tied up and planned to check his skull. We found him convulsing. He had eaten about an hour earlier and he seemed fine then, but now he seemed to be having something like an epileptic seizure. We untied him and placed him face down making sure he did not swallow his tongue and we held his flailing arms and legs. Maggie brought the detector close to his skull and we detected an acute screeching sound. Betty, who was also our base medic, ran to the triage container, and returned with a bottle of antiseptic, a bandage and a small scalpel. She searched all over Bob's skull for the sensor, and found the small lump behind the left ear and cut into it to remove the sensor. Afterward she cleaned the wound and applied pressure. By then Bob had stopped convulsing. The sensor that Leticia picked up and held in her hand continued to emit this high piercing sound that one could hear when placed near the skull. Betty bandaged Bob up, gave him a shot of antibiotic and something to knock him out. Thirty minutes later the sensor had stopped emitting, but we didn't know if that was good or bad. Bob was still unresponsive; we restrained him in his bunk and decided to check back on him later.

Back in the dining room we started going over what had taken place and what to do next. Bob was a control freak. Clearly he had not been transmitting the regular monitor feed to the Lab people in the few days that we had had him tied up. So, they had to know something was up. They had to figure that either there was something wrong with Bob or that he had become part of a conspiracy. To ensure that he reported back as mandated, he was sent that warning.

— What could be happening? Whatever that sensor in his head was doing it sure stir-fried Bob's wiring.

— They probably wanted to force him to talk. After that kind of auditory torture I would answer whatever they asked.

— That's for sure. Ay!

— All right, we'll see what happens with Bob later; right now we need to hear about the reaction to our plan from the mining camp. Who all was there?

Frank and Jake reported that, as we had thought, we could not count on the pilots, Lab researchers, or compound security team. Only one of the Lab assistants would even talk to Tom when he visited the Lab, but Marcy was not the type to get involved since she was a graduate student working on her dissertation research and feared being sent home before completion or who knows what. That research came first, was what she said. She saw whatever complaint we might have as a labor issue and was afraid to have anything to do with it. The last time Tom had been at the Lab and asked about her bank account back on Earth, to see if she was getting credited, she didn't want to talk about it. She even suggested a meeting with the Lab director, who would undoubtedly convey our concerns to the Houston Center. If something was going on, she did not really want to know the details. What was also clear was that the Lab researchers were unreachable; they would no more talk to a miner or a Teco than to a homeless person.

— So much for that, but the really interesting thing was that there were two Chinese colonists at the meeting. One was involved in a mining project and the other in laboratory research. The researcher had not found it beneath him to attend a meeting of the Cone Crater alliance, or the Latter Day Maquis, as we started calling ourselves jokingly after that. The Chinese, for their part, had no plans to return to Earth. In fact, they were interested in expanding their colonies, were bringing up their families, and trying to increase the number of trips between China and the Moon to bring supplies, instruments, tools, and other basics. They had started building large pavilion centers that could house up to a hundred people . Their government was not interested in killing off their workers but in increasing their number by shipping more up. Already their gardening efforts were having some success with their hydroponic nurseries. In time they hoped to bring children up as well and that would imply building even larger housing centers. Their mining efforts were paying off and being used as fuels on the moon itself. They thought that, at most, within a hundred years, the Chinese colonies would be self sufficient. That was the goal and they made it known to us that we would be welcome at their colonies, if we decided to escape our camps. But if we insisted on returning to Earth, all they could do was supply us with a few weapons. At that point they pulled out some five old fashioned pistols that probably wouldn't even work up here anyhow and two particle beam rifles, that we hoped would. After more questions than answers, our Chinese guests joined us for a meal and left. They had a long ride back, although theirs would not be done solely on land as their vehicles could also attain low levels of altitude, almost like gliders catching the sandstorm waves, that made their travel much faster. Even so, it would take a full two earth days to get back to their base camps.

— After the Chinese left, we knew we had to make a decision and it was up to us, the 30 miners and 7 or 8 Tecos, to carry out our plan or not. What we came up with was this: shuttle transport from the orbiting ship will be arriving in two days. So, it will be crucial for us all to arrive at the Transport Center the day that the shuttles return with supplies. The rendezvous ship will remain in orbit for a little over 24 hours awaiting the shuttles' return several hours later with the cargo of rocks and minerals. Depending on the load, sometimes more than one shuttle trip is necessary, and given the particular tilt of this orbit, that means the ship goes by every 8 hours or so. The Lab is naturally expecting a group of miners to arrive to pick up their supplies and some new instruments that Tom requested to facilitate the detection of particular minerals. The packs will require the assistance of three or four men in two lunar jeeps to carry back the load. But instead of 4 miners, 29 will be arriving in five jeeps. Miner #30, the spy Ted and his baseball cap, wouldn't be leaving the Moon, it was agreed.

— From our base camp, they'll of course be expecting Bob for the supply pick up, but the eight of us will arrive. We will drive there in our three jeeps. We can't all show up at the same time, or our arrival will set off an alarm. That is why it will be important for only 4 miners and two disposal workers to arrive at first, seemingly just to pick up supplies. That will guarantee our entry into the lab and into the center, and access to the warehouse for supplies. For these six individuals to take over the space Com Center and Lab, they will need to disarm the six members of the security team or kill them, whichever comes first. The guards are generally posted outside the Lab, outside the Communication Center, and outside the warehouse. Since we have only five pistols of dubious capabilities and two laser rifles, the six of us will be armed and the extra rifle will be in the hands of the miners, just in case anything happens so that those in the rear will have a means of defending themselves and advancing, por si las dudas. We will also have other types of weapons, especially the explosives the miners have. Once we control the three sites, we will take the Lab supervisors prisoners as well as their assistants, the three pilots, and the security guards; we will demand to speak with Director Johnson to find out what specifically happened to the prior teams and where the orders to terminate them came from.

Frank and Jake stressed that in order to carry all this out, it would be important to prevent any communication between the Lab and the orbiting ship or the Houston Center. That is why the first thing had to be to take control of the Com Center. Frank and I would see to that. Once the security guards were out of the way and we had control of all communications, we needed to be able to contact the rest of the mining and Tech crews that would be at the periphery of the Lab, near enough to be on site 10 minutes after the first group arrived. Once both we and the miners were in, the next thing was to destroy the communication system and disrupt the satellite transmitter. The miners would be in charge of that task. We would assist in disabling the antenna and the satellite dish on the north end of the transport center landing pad.

There was a bit of relief in knowing that, if need be, we could always seek asylum with the Chinese, but that wasn't our goal. We were hopeful our risky plan to return to Earth would work out. The problem then became how to handle the Bob question. We decided to wait to see what he said when he woke up. We spent the rest of the time preparing. It was decided that Frank and Sam would be the team members sent presumably for the supplies. Both knew how to use a gun. Sam however did not know enough about computers to help disable the communication system. For this reason, the plan was changed and it was decided that I should go along, although I would not be armed, unless we came up with another weapon. Once we took over the Lab and Com Center, we needed to make sure that the shuttles were fueled up, on deck, and that the pilots were under restraints. Of course we knew that they could also communicate via their shuttles, but we counted on their being in their rooms resting up after the previous day's flights. Part of the prisoner taking would involve going into the dorms across from the warehouse and next to the com lab. Lab supervisors and their assistants had their quarters within the lab building itself. So, it was a matter of keeping them there and unable to communicate out. The miners were to split into three units: those helping out by securing the Lab, those going to the warehouse, and those commandeering the shuttles. The Com Center was the linchpin of the whole operation and it was strictly our baby and we had to concentrate all our efforts there, o nos llevaba la chingada.

Black holes. What are they, you ask. Well, they are collapsed stars, stars sort of like our sun, let's say, that die out. The stars are always burning and it is this combustion that produces the light that we see. It is produced by a nuclear fusion process that converts hydrogen into helium. The larger the star, the faster the hydrogen will burn until it burns out in a few million years. As the fuel runs out, to put it in an understandable way, the star begins to contract upon itself until it produces a total collapse with an incredible density, an infinite density, that produces a singularity and sucks up everything around it. I can best explain it by reminding you about how light emitted by a star travels though space. That light is what we see on Earth and may have been emitted millions of years ago. But in the case of the formation of a singularity, no light can escape that density. What happens is that in the case of a singularity the light emitted by helium curves back into itself and not outwardly because the gravity of the black hole is so intense. That is what is called a black hole. So, how do we know it exists if it does not emit light? That's actually a very good question, Pedro. We know because the mass of that black hole retains its satellites in orbit. The galaxies all orbit around these gigantic black holes. So, we know the black hole is there by its effect on other masses in space. And then there are also the voids in space. We still don't know anything about them.

Some six hours later Bob regained consciousness and when he realized he was in his cubicle he got up screaming: "No more, please, no more." When we were finally able to calm him down a bit, he began telling us that the Lab Supervisors had come to suspect that he was neglecting his surveillance and communication duties, attributing it to his becoming involved with one of the female disposal crew members on our team. To encourage him to correct that behavior, they had activated his cranial sensor. Still groggy, he touched the nape of his neck and around his ear and found a patch and a bandage under his hair. It was then that we explained what had happened, how we had found him convulsing. He said he preferred to die rather than suffer through that again, to hear that eerie high pitch sound that seemed to be rupturing his ear drum. Bob then said we could count on him for anything. He fell back asleep or unconscious, we weren't sure, but knowing that the implant had been removed.

— Bob, were all the Lab people there when they x-ed them out?

— Everyone, except the Lab Assistants. I guess they didn't trust them too much.

Bob put us on the spot. No one really trusted him. On the one hand, we knew that he would be killed if we left him behind. On the other hand, we recognized he could be useful in the Lab assault at least initially, as his presence would make dealing with the supervisors, researchers and security guards easier. Once in, we'd see how things went. So, we decided to sedate him and take him with us on the jeeps. If we died, we would all die. If we made it, we would all make it.

Bob received a message from the Lab Center a bit later. Betty answered it: "Our com officer has suffered an epileptic seizure. I gave him a tranquilizer and he seems to be doing better. He has slept for the last eight hours. When he awakens, he will contact you with an update. - Betty Fraser."

— So, what was the whole "Black Hole War" about, Mom? I don't get it.

— Well, Pedro, it's rather complicated. It's still going on. I'm not sure I understand it well myself, but the gist of it is that there has always been this antagonism between macro explanations of the universe, that deal with planets, stars, the curvature of space, black holes, etc., as described in Einstein's general theory of relativity, for example, and micro explanations, like those of quantum mechanics. How to unite these two conceptions of reality has been and continues to be the trick. In the 21st century there was a quantum theorist named Susskind who challenged the work of another physicist named Hawking. Hawking argued that black holes suck up everything in their wake to produce a density, a singularity, where nothing seemingly escapes; all that energy, however, is dissipated through the radiation of heat. Hawking also implied that in black hole evaporation all information is lost. Susskind, on the other hand, a quantum mechanics theorist and one of the founders of string theory, could not accept that. He insisted that information leaked out in the radiation of heat. From his analysis of the black hole in terms of a three-dimensional projection of a hologram he conjectured that our universe is similarly a three-dimensional projection of a two-dimensional layer of information. Whether notions of holographic projections of information will explain different dimensions, branes, and give us a broader explanation of reality is something that physicists continue to work on. It is something that you too can aspire to do, Pedro. And after you come to understand it, perhaps you can explain it to me, cause at this point I'm a bit lost.

・・・》》》》》》♪ ♪ ● ● ● ● ● ●

The day before we planned to take over the lab, Maggie had another dream.

— Did you wake up screaming again.

— No, this time I was just shaking all over and I couldn't stop.

— What happened?

— I dreamt we had gotten to the Lab and gone straight to the Director's office, but there was no one there. We then tried the Com Center, but it too was empty. At the dining area we turned on the lights and sensors and it was then that we saw the rippling effect near the back wall. We all froze and stared at what looked like a tear in space and time. That's when Sam saw them.

— Hey, everybody. C'mere.

He was standing before what looked like a mirror or screen. The ripple effect was concentrated there. We looked and looked till we saw them, the Director and Lab Researchers, beyond our time-space, in another brane or dimension.

— What the hell!!

— Where are they? There's nothing but a wall there.

— Oh, m'god. Look at what happens when they turn.

— They seem to be working in a Lab beyond here.

— But look at their heads

That's when we saw that they had grasshopper-like heads. We all started backing out of there as fast as we could. I was still shaking when I woke up.

— What do you think it means?

— It's just your anxiety. Don't worry. It'll be all right. Although it wouldn't surprise me if we learned that they were working on manipulating the branes in space in that damned Lab.

— Girl, you have some bad ass dreams, said Sam, nodding his head side to side.

〉〉〉〉〉▶▶●●●●●

We now had the perfect explanation for Bob's failure to go himself after the supplies. The miners arrived a few hours later with their instruments, wire, wirecutters, pliers, knives, and Z-5 explosive charges, which worked in low gravity. In the meantime, Sam had searched in Bob's cubicle and found another weapon. Now all three of us from the Teco team involved in the first assault would be armed. We all had extra bullets as well, extra oxygen tanks and extra batteries. Betty gave Bob a shot that put him out of commission for the duration. We put on his suit and placed him in the back seat of one of the jeeps with Betty, with Jake driving. The second jeep would be driven by Maggie and Leticia. In the back we placed our supplies. The third jeep was driven by me with Frank and Sam as the passengers. We would go in first to purportedly pick up the supplies for our base camp. The five mining jeeps were also fully loaded. Two of the miners joined our jeeps, one went with Maggie and Leticia and one with Jake, Betty and Bob. That meant that the lead miners' jeep had only four members, as agreed upon, but ours had three rather than two. Frank explained the change in setup to Tom as better for technical aspects of the dismantling of the com system once we were in.

 We were all suited up and we left the lunar base as if we were returning in a few hours. We had even left our music cells. Still, I remembered the lines: "Against the Wind. We were young and strong, we were running against the wind." I think they were burnt into my brain after hearing that song so many times.

 Yes, Pedro Pedrín, in the end it all turned out, more or less, as we'd planned. Otherwise I wouldn't be here to tell the tale and you certainly wouldn't be here. The surprise attack worked out.

 They were not expecting us. They assumed we were there to pick up supplies. Two of the guards fired upon the jeeps after they saw us go into the Com Center and we had to take them out, but the others were surprised and taken without any resistance. They didn't even have time to sound the alarm. The soundproofing kept the gunshots from being heard in the labs. Only the pilots woke up but the miners broke in and took them hostage. Frank, Sam, and I took over the Com Center after tying up one of the assistants who was receiving transmissions from the orbiting craft. Jake and a couple of the miners were able to take control of the shuttles as well and radioed back to the orbiter that in some eight hours we would be rendezvousing with them with a cargo of rocks. Over and out.

We set the Z-5 charges on the antenna and satellite dish to explode after we took off on the shuttles. We took the Director and other researchers hostage, together with the lab assistants, pilots and guards. They were all taken to the dining room where we confronted them with our findings. We tried to make them talk, to explain who had given the order to kill us and the previous crews, but silence was their only response. The miners proposed lynching them right there; give us something to do to kill time before the shuttles are launched, they argued. Frank said we should throw them out without their space suits so that they could suffer like his brother Peter had. We tied them all up and began a search of their computers to see what orders had come from Houston Control. The more explicit orders had been deleted from their files but not one brief message of congratulations sent around the time of our arrival: "Well done, Johnson. These metals are more valuable than a thousand disposal techs. Excellent cost/benefit analysis. Proceed."

We went into the space hangar where the shuttles were located and began to talk about the next step. We'd left two of the miners guarding the prisoners. Returning to Houston was out of the question. That was clear. We had under eight hours to decide what to do with the prisoners. In the meantime we needed to remove all the cargo from the shuttles to make room for our surprise passenger shipment. We planned to leave in the shuttles to rendezvous with the orbiting ship as soon as it came close enough again. Leticia proposed we hold a court hearing. We had all seen the corpses, either of miners or waste disposal workers, so by all rights the hearing would not take long. Those of us at the waste disposal site base had heard Bob's testimony, though he of course was knocked out. Ted, the spy at the mining camp, had also confessed, but he could not be called to appear because he was already dead; the other miners had taken care of that detail. We could also point to the e-mails and other messages that explicitly or implicitly acknowledged what had been going on. We decided to carry out the hearing since we still had some six hours to wait. We selected Tom as the judge and the jury was composed of six miners and six Tecos. The four lab assistants, who had not been directly involved in the deaths of the workers, were taken to a dorm room, tied up, and locked in. After hearing all the evidence, our jury left to

deliberate in an adjoining room. Throughout the presentation of evidence, the director Johnson assumed an air of superiority and looked down at us as if we were imbeciles.

While the jury deliberated, we provided the accused with food, a variety of dried goods that we found on hand, and beer. The jury returned, having found the lab director, lab researchers, guards, and pilots, including the one who had shot Peter, all guilty. But the accused did not respond to the verdict; they seemed to be asleep. They were, in fact, dead, poisoned just like the miners and Tecos had been.

Nobody appeared to be shocked by the sight of the 14 "sleeping" diners, nor did anyone ask what had happened or who had done it or anything of the kind. The only question seemed to be, "what's next?"

— I can't get over how stupid they must have thought we were. Do you realize that they figured we would never find out what was going on?

— That's the way it looks, Frank. Arrogance, plain and simple. OK, so now what do we do with the bodies?

— I think we ought to take them to the mine pits where the miners are buried.

— Well, I think we should place them in sealed containers, like the murdered Tecos.

— Let's be practical here, folks. We do not have time to return to either site and be back here to rendezvous with the ship in a few hours.

— Well, then, let's bury them nearby, in the area that is being cleared for expanding the landing strip. In fact, we can make a hole with our robotic excavators, place them inside and blow the hole. Once on the ship, if they ask about the blast, we'll tell them the miners were helping to clear the area for the new landing strip.

hat's in fact what we did. After the explosion, the hole caved into itself, sort of imploding and filling up with sand and the rocky granules that make up the lunar surface. The area looked as if it had always been so, perfectly lunar, and the entire operation took no more than 3 or 4 hours.

We then returned to the space center. Only the four lab assistants who had arrived after Team 4 and had not been involved were still alive. I did ask myself whose idea it was to use the poison, but I never voiced the question. Actually, none of us asked because we all agreed that poetic justice required that they go out the same way as all of our worker brothers had gone. I remembered the famous lines: "Fuenteovejuna lo hizo." You'll have to read some old Spanish plays from the Golden Age, Pedro, to see what that line is about. In any event, we threw away the poisoned food and cleaned up, just in case some poor soul came through desperate for food. We made copies of messages that pertained to the disappearance of the waste workers and miners; we already had the digital shots of the corpses that Leticia had taken. We decided to take the lab assistants back with us, in restraints, as witnesses and hostages at least, till we reached Earth. Then we'd play it by ear.

About an hour later we received word from the orbiter indicating they had been trying to reach us. We answered that we had suffered some com problems but that we would rendezvous with them in an hour at the assigned coordinates with our load.

It was decided that Jeb, Sam and Tom would pilot our shuttles. All three had been pilots before and had applied for the space program, but they had been rejected because they lacked graduate degrees. No doubt since Sam and Jeb were black and Tom was Latino, there just might've been some racism involved as well. In any case, they had not been deemed acceptable candidates. The more we talked about it, the less we were convinced that three shuttles should go up. We then decided not to take the risk of taking three shuttles; two would be enough, lest we encounter any problems. The key thing now was for the first shuttle to arrive, control the docking bay and nauts to ensure that the orbiter would receive the second shuttle. There were now a total of 41 individuals to be ferried up to the orbiter; we divided up into 21 and 20 per shuttle with Sam and Jeb as pilots.

When the two shuttles rendezvoused, one of the nauts opened the cargo door and asked the suited pilot to begin unloading the payload. Since it was all done with robotic instruments it was relatively easy for one person to do. The naut turned to open the second cargo door and gave the other pilot a similar order. When he turned around, he saw not cargo but people climbing into the cargo bay.

— What the... What's going on? Who are these people? This is supposed to be a payload transport. Where are the other pilots?

— They're back at the lab. We had a bit of a problem with the pilots, sort of an insubordination problem; that's why we had to make some changes; we also have orders to return to Earth. No explanation given. Maybe it's a matter of international relations. Who knows? In any case we're supposed to return and land not in Houston or California, but in Yucatán, the center from which we left.

— But, Yucatán is always used as a takeoff center, because of the force field erected there, but it is never used as a landing site.

— Look, those are the orders. That's what we were told through an encrypted communication and we were told not to link up again with them until we land in Yucatán. I don't know what's up either, but orders are orders, right?

Once we were all on board, the cargo bay doors we closed and the shuttles sent back down to the surface of tl moon by remote control. The cargo bay was reconverted int a passenger area; all the crew seats had been folded up t make space for the cargo. We had second thoughts about the nauts who all this time had known full well the previous crews were not being returned to Earth, about the supplies that continued to be strictly for a small number of workers. Tom and Sam went up to the navigation control module and began questioning them. As expected, they denied knowing anything about anything. Their job was to fly in and out and not ask questions. If they had ever wondered about the disposal techs, they had deemed it none of their business. They were just professional astronauts, that was all. In fact, they didn't want to know what we were doing on board. Sam and Tom decided to sit behind them to ensure 1) that we would not be met by an army and 2) that the heading was set for the Yucatán station.

We took our helmets off after a while and tried to make ourselves comfortable. As we approached the Earth's atmosphere we would need to put them on again and grab on as best we could since the cabin was fitted with seats for no more than 20 passengers and there were 41 of us on board.

Houston Control began asking why they had no communication with the lunar lab and asked the space craft already in orbit if it had any news. The nauts replied that they had picked up the cargo and were on their way back. We also had them relay that the lab had indicated previously that it was having some com problems but that they were working on them. It would probably take a few hours to fix. The nauts complied; they had clearly decided they wanted to survive this flight and not asking questions was their prime directive. To ensure no further contact the nauts decided not to contact the space station in orbit and so we began our trip back through space.

ht that much of the universe is "dark matter," much as 90%. This matter is not directly visible but about it because of its gravitational pull. The of this dark matter was discovered or detected when ted that the speed of some stars orbiting on the outer ions of spiral galaxies, like our own Milky Way, at times, to be exceedingly fast, faster than would be le for the stars to continue to be held in orbit unless was a greater gravitational attraction than that provided he visible galaxies that they orbit. This discrepancy gests the presence of additional matter that we do not rceive. In fact, galaxies contain 5 to 10 times more matter an we can see. It is thought that this dark matter may be different from the matter we know. What we don't know is whether this dark matter will be enough to slow down the expansion of the universe. This invisible mass could also be evidence of other dimensions or shadow worlds. These shadow worlds or dimensions are called "branes," and some speculate that there could be a variety of "shadow branes." Physicists are also theorizing the existence of "dark energy." There is much to learn about what seems to be an ever-expanding universe, but, of course, we may be wrong on many, if not most, counts. Only future research will tell and maybe you, Pedro, will be part of it.

⁙))))) ▶ ▶ ● ● ● ● ● ●

The re-entry proved to be a horrible experience, mostly because we were not properly restrained, but we did the best we could to tie ourselves down. As we approached the atmosphere Houston Control indicated we should land in California. Our naut answered that we had secret orders to land in Yucatán, to which the control center replied that there was presently a hurricane in the Caribbean and that landing there was not advisable.

Where to land was the issue that we had been discussing since coming on board. If we returned to Houston or California and they suspected why we had returned and if

— So, what was the whole "Black Hole War" about, Mom? I don't get it.

— *Well, Pedro, it's rather complicated. It's still going on. I'm not sure I understand it well myself, but the gist of it is that there has always been this antagonism between macro explanations of the universe, that deal with planets, stars, the curvature of space, black holes, etc., as described in Einstein's general theory of relativity, for example, and micro explanations, like those of quantum mechanics. How to unite these two conceptions of reality has been and continues to be the trick. In the 21st century there was a quantum theorist named Susskind who challenged the work of another physicist named Hawking. Hawking argued that black holes suck up everything in their wake to produce a density, a singularity, where nothing seemingly escapes; all that energy, however, is dissipated through the radiation of heat. Hawking also implied that in black hole evaporation all information is lost. Susskind, on the other hand, a quantum mechanics theorist and one of the founders of string theory, could not accept that. He insisted that information leaked out in the radiation of heat. From his analysis of the black hole in terms of a three-dimensional projection of a hologram he conjectured that our universe is similarly a three-dimensional projection of a two-dimensional layer of information. Whether notions of holographic projections of information will explain different dimensions, branes, and give us a broader explanation of reality is something that physicists continue to work on. It is something that you too can aspire to do, Pedro. And after you come to understand it, perhaps you can explain it to me, cause at this point I'm a bit lost.*

〉〉〉〉〉♦♦♦●●●●

The day before we planned to take over the lab, Maggie had another dream.

— Did you wake up screaming again.

— No, this time I was just shaking all over and I couldn't stop.

— What happened?

— I dreamt we had gotten to the Lab and gone straight to the Director's office, but there was no one there. We then tried the Com Center, but it too was empty. At the dining area we turned on the lights and sensors and it was then that we saw the rippling effect near the back wall. We all froze and stared at what looked like a tear in space and time. That's when Sam saw them.

— Hey, everybody. C'mere.

He was standing before what looked like a mirror or screen. The ripple effect was concentrated there. We looked and looked till we saw them, the Director and Lab Researchers, beyond our time-space, in another brane or dimension.

— What the hell!!

— Where are they? There's nothing but a wall there.

— Oh, m'god. Look at what happens when they turn.

— They seem to be working in a Lab beyond here.

— But look at their heads

That's when we saw that they had grasshopper-like heads. We all started backing out of there as fast as we could. I was still shaking when I woke up.

— What do you think it means?

— It's just your anxiety. Don't worry. It'll be all right. Although it wouldn't surprise me if we learned that they were working on manipulating the branes in space in that damned Lab.

— Girl, you have some bad ass dreams, said Sam, nodding his head side to side.

))))))♦♦●●●●

We now had the perfect explanation for Bob's failure to go himself after the supplies. The miners arrived a few hours later with their instruments, wire, wirecutters, pliers, knives, and Z-5 explosive charges, which worked in low gravity. In made our escape. When asked what had happened to the lab supervisors, we simply said they had been left behind, waiting to be found by Houston Control. We had all sworn not to tell. Since the lab assistants had not been present at the trial, final meal, nor at the burial, they had no knowledge of what had transpired, whatever they might suspect.

The commandeered ship was in time returned to the Houston Center. We made it clear that the two nauts had been forced to land us in Tierra del Fuego. Once out, our reports to the World Human Rights Commission caused a scandal, of course, and a special commission of WHRC investigators was sent to the Moon a few weeks later to verify our report. They found the corpses in the sealed containers and in the mining pits, just as we had stated. Autopsies were conducted proving that they had been poisoned just as we had declared, except for Peter, who had been shot after his organs exploded. If they ever found the dead lab supervisors and pilots, we do not know; nothing was ever reported. The government of Cali-Texas expressed, of course, its shock and dismay at what had happened, as if they knew nothing of it. In the end NIO intervened saying it too was shocked and promising to insure events like these would never happen again, the usual pendejadas. But at least we knew that the other lunar colonies had become aware of what had happened to us and were wary; and perhaps now there would be a guarantee of their workers' return. Cali-Texas also knew, from our declarations, that the Chinese colonies also were aware of what had happened in our camps and, of course that was what most bothered NIO. A few months later, when we were already here in Chinganaza, between Loja and Iquitos, we discovered that our salaries had just been transferred into our accounts. At least that enabled my parents and your Aunt Lupita to finally leave the Reservation. Who would have thought we'd end up in a place called Chinganaza?

By the way, we found out later that Ushuaia had once been a penal colony and that a good many of the things in the old part of town had been built by prison labor. How ironic, don't you think, that we would end up on a landing strip with cholo roots.

>>>>>>●●●●●

— Maggie and I, we love you dearly. Your parents are our best friends and don't forget that I carried you in my womb for 9 months. You are our son as well, in so many ways. I can't tell you to look up our folks when you return as they would probably shut the door in your face, as they did to us, but I have a baby sister, now about 20 years old, Lauren Trejo; if you should ever meet her, perhaps she'll want to hear about me, about what we did here and on the Moon, about who we became. Perhaps she too has come to rebel against my parents' reactionary views. It's a wild hope but I suppose hope is the last thing to go. Take care, Pedro.

>>>>>>●●●●●

In time, NIO and Cali-Texas sent their own ship to the Moon with yet another commission to investigate; they also found the collected bodies in the containers as well as the lab and shuttles. In time we heard too that our kidnapped lab assistants returned to the moon with new supervisors running the operation. New mining workers were sent to the Exochev Mining Camp, this time with guarantees of safe return. Our pavilions were abandoned and new dump sites created. When the new crew of waste disposal workers returned, after their contracts were up, much was made in the press about their safe return, their contributions, the importance of the lunar project, blah, blah, blah.

None of us have ever returned to Cali-Texas, at least not yet; all our subsequent declarations to the press and before the World Human Rights Commissions were made in the South. At first, while we were within the Southern Confederation we had the protection of the government, but afterwards, when things died down and everything returned to its usual "normalcy," some of us began to feel the persecution and the threats. We were under constant surveillance by satellite and on the surface.

⟨·⟩⟩⟩⟩▸▸▸●●●●●

We arrived at the Iguazú Hotel after leaving the southern tip of Argentina, first by way of Buenos Aires and then on to Iguazú, where we could more easily go from Argentina to Brazil or Paraguay, if need be. Bob stayed in Buenos Aires and some of the miners left for Brazil. The rest of us stayed together for a while till Bill left for Mexico. In Iguazú we were in contact with an anarcho group that was setting up a global communication center linking anti-capitalist movements throughout the world. Since Frank and I had skills in that area, we joined their center and it was there that we met Guamán the Elder. He told us about their commons in Chinganaza and despite the name it sounded rather utopian, too good to be true, but all of us were eager to hear more. We invited him to meet with our group and tell us more about it. We however ended up having to go underground when two of the miners were found dead in a Brazilian hotel. A month after we had left Buenos Aires, Bob was also found dead in the Argentine capital. He had been knifed and his body thrown beside the road in the outskirts of the city. Gallows humor allowed the remaining members to joke about our clandestine status. We feared we would be followed and killed off one by one. We knew then that we were targets, probably of the Space Center in Cali-Texas that had its hitmen and were out to shut us up, now that the initial uproar over our declarations was over and people had moved on to other news items. We received a message on our compact one evening while Guamán the Elder was there, warning us that we were next. It was then that the Elder suggested we leave with him for Chinganaza, located in the southeastern part of Ecuador, the Amazon jungle area reclaimed by Ecuador from Peru in 2050 and populated mostly by displaced indigenous tribes who had managed to claim the area as an ancestral homeland and establish a commune here, returning to their communal agricultural practices. Here, Guamán the Elder said, we would be safe. That's when we decided to join the commons, where you were born.

〉〉〉〉〉〉●●●●●●

— I'm leaving you this tiny pouch of Moon sand. It says: "To my Pedro from his Maggie." Keep it as a token of our love and hopes for you as a future astronaut or astronomer. Leticia and I will stay close to your parents; you can bet on that and we'll think of you always. Whenever there's a chance, we'll send word. Take good care of the iguana for me and don't forget to put food out for our bird friends. Be good to Betty; she'll be missing us tons. Give her a hug for us every once in a while and mind Tom. You and Guamancito can be a handful at times. No venturing out into the jungle without Tom and Betty. Promise me. Love you lots. Stay safe and Happy Birthday.

〉〉〉〉〉〉●●●●●●

How to attain social change? We've gone over this subject time and time again. Before going to the Moon and while I was involved with the anarcho group, I thought, like Gabriel and my brother Ricardo, that what was important was making the people of Cali-Texas aware of what was happening. Consciousness-raising, a tactic tried centuries before by feminists and others, was to be our main strategy. For this a variety of tactics could be used. The distribution of leaflets, pamphlets and such, however, was no longer possible from Chinganaza. The web was our primary means to make contact with the world, but as time went on the state came to control the internet as well. There were still clandestine sites but those were not the ones that most people tapped. Still we spent time setting up websites with information on what was going on. In the past our other tactic had been that of agit-prop, creating acts of disturbance that often were publicized in the press, on television, and on state news sites on the web. These acts at least made people aware that there was resistance somewhere, somehow. The state often used these demonstrations to restrict freedoms further, but that, we figured, only upset the population more and created tensions that we hoped would lead to an explosion. Back then we bided our time through this war of position. But now, we've had to recognize that these discursive and agit-prop acts did not lead to much, much less to an insurrection. Almost fifteen years have passed since Gabriel and I were arrested and still things remain the same. The Reservations are still operating with a stranglehold on the working class, mostly of Latinos, African Americans and poor Whites and Asians. It's time for a new strategy. It's time for something else. Perhaps it's time for a new version of the old urban guerrilla tactics that were declared defunct two centuries ago. What is definitely clear is that we have to propose something new when we arrive back in Cali-Texas at the new international underground anti-capitalist conference.

○ ⟩ ⟩ ⟩ ⟩ ▸ ▸ ● ● ● ● ●

The day we were to leave Chinganaza for SanTijuana, Maggie had another dream. It was Leticia who told me about it.

— She woke up screaming again.

— What's going on?

— She said she dreamt we had gone to Macas again and were going up the volcano, up Sangay. Here she comes now.

— Hey, Maggie, Come have some breakfast. Another strange dream?

— Who told you? Ah, Leticia, of course. Well, this time it was a doozy.

— Tell me.

— You remember when we all went up to Macas about 6 months ago through the road from Guamote and after a day's rest traveled on up to the Sangay mountain? Well, in my dream Leticia and I were with the group trying to go up the mountain, but we never made it to the top. From where we stopped, however, it was high enough to see Chimborazo and Tungurahua in the distance. It was impressive. On the other side was the jungle and we could also see the Río Pastaza. Just like on our trip. When we looked up we could also see a reddish halo at the top of Sangay but this time it slowly became redder and redder and then purple and blue as ash started to rain on us. Instead of descending the mountain we all decided to climb higher but then the ash turned heavier and we saw rivulets of lava coming down and then rocks and boulders. That's when I screamed and I heard Leticia saying, "Wake up. Wake up."

— You're right about one thing. What we propose to do is like climbing up to the very top of Sangay, but what will rain down on us will not be ash and rocks but bullets, probably. Still, you'll have to admit that was one great trip we took to Sangay. Now when I think of it I will probably recall your nightmare.

— Sorry.

⁂

Yes, we fled here together, our entire team, well, except for Bob. We had to all travel incognito to the Amazon jungle. Actually we're in an area close to where your father Gabriel died. Besides it's one of the few places in the world where the jungle still exists and where communal farming is the primary practice. Tom and Jeb also joined us, as did Bill, for a while anyhow, before he moved on to Mexico. The other miners decided it was prudent to disappear, to not be associated with us, to try to blend into the crowd in some big city. I think one ended up in China. Since most of the workers were Black, Latino or Asian, they have been able to keep a low profile. We haven't heard about any more deaths of any other workers from our groups, although we are not really much in touch, for obvious reasons. It's not been good.

・・・・・・・・・・・・・・

It became clear in our discussions at night in Chinganaza that change had to come through struggles within the cholo Reservations. Several of us in the group, both -ex Techs and ex-miners came from Reservation backgrounds. There are now Reservations in Texas, in New Mexico, in Arizona, in California, in Utah, in Colorado, in Oregon, and in Washington. There are also Reservations in Chihuahua and Nuevo Leon. Once we had come to some major decisions, we began to establish contact with groups within all of these sites. That was nine years ago, shortly after Pedro was born. Through the years there have been a few meetings in Coahuila and Baja with delegates from the Reservations, that is, with residents of the Res'es that have had trusty positions and could go in and out without any problem. There are inside CaliTexas non-Res groups from La prole as well interested in helping out, especially with the procurement of weapons. Plans have been set in motion and we are now eager to return and become involved.

This is not merely a personal thing, not an individual battle, although I have much to resent. It will be a collective struggle, a class struggle. What Pacomio tried to do oh so many centuries ago, the Indians in Chinganaza have achieved and now we too must attain this freedom from exploitation on the reservations in Cali-Texas. Chinganaza will serve as an inspiration for future changes in Cali-Texas. Our struggle will be the beginning of a different world.

"I found myself seeking shelter against the wind." I still remember the song. I know you've heard it a million times, but there's a reason I keep coming back to it. I can't get it out of my head, I guess, because, in some melodramatic yet cynical way, it seems to be the story of my life, no, our lives, and I guess, yours too. Our arrival here in this isolated indigenous area is another story. Your father Frank and I became a real couple after coming back to Earth. We had been through so much together and we were really tight, but somehow had not thought of ourselves as a couple till we got here and were able to live relatively without fear, although the feeling of apprehension has never entirely left us. When we tried to have a baby, we found that we could not. Apparently the nuclear particles that rained down on us on a daily basis on the Moon had made both of us sterile. That's when I remembered the frozen fertilized eggs in storage in Mexico. After making contact with my brother Ricardo through some contacts in Chile, I found out that he actually had continued to pay the maintenance charge for the embryo repository somewhere on some rancho east of Toluca on a monthly basis and that Gabriel's and my embryos were still available to me.

 Right, exactly, that's why when you were little, I'd sometimes call you my "huevito ranchero." And that's why we decided to name you Pedro Gabriel to remind us —and you— of what came before you. Anyhow, to make a long story short, I could not conceive nor carry a baby to full term, but it turned out that Leticia could; for some reason she had not been affected. She and Maggie were still a couple as were Tom and Betty. Sam and Jake ended up partnering with two Ecuadorian women and live on the outskirts of Chinganaza. The rest of us live in this commune, where we work together; here the land belongs to those who work it; everything is shared and there are no bosses, but we're not fooling ourselves; we are a tiny bubble in a turbulent world.

A few months after I contacted my brother, Leticia traveled to Chile where she was met by Ricardo with the frozen embryos. They went together to a fertility clinic in Valparaíso, where Leticia was impregnated. Ricardo returned to Cali-Texas and Leticia came back home. Nine months later a beautiful boy was born, you, Pedro Gabriel, my huevito ranchero, my son. Pedrín, you are as much my son as Frank's, Leticia's, Maggie's, Tom's and Betty's. Betty and Tom, upon finding that Betty too could not conceive, decided to adopt an orphaned baby boy, an indigenous child, Little Guamán, your buddy. Having a child was a difficult decision for me. Back what seems a lifetime ago, when we conceived you, Gabriel and I were hoping for a different world, a better future, but as you can see, we are all still struggling. We are all still "running against the wind." Like we've told you, Frank and I will be going away for a bit; you'll be safe here with Tom and Betty. We're going north, where we'll join others that want to bring about change. The world is a dangerous place, Pedro, but we'll try to be back for your next birthday. That's why I've been telling you all this. These are things you need to know, so that you too can face the wind.

))))))) ● ● ● ● ●

I received these memoirs from Bill in Mexico several months after my Mom and Dad reached SanTijuana. After that, the two of them, as well as our other friends, disappeared and we haven't had any communication from any of them since. We've all heard about the social upheaval that broke out three years after they left Chinganaza and that is still going on in Cali-Texas. It's been eight long years and still no word, not even from you, Uncle Ricardo. Every birthday I look for a message, something. I need to know they're still alive.

Betty and Tom have been really good to me and Guamán is like a brother to me, but things here in Chinganaza are starting to disintegrate, what with the desperate need for uncontaminated lands that has led millions to want to move south, especially to live near what is left of the Amazonian forests. With the arrival of hundreds of thousands of new settlers in the Andean region, the Indians are again being dispossessed of the little they had regained back in the twenty-first century and the unique biodiversity of the region is again being destroyed. It is becoming a new site of struggle. Already hundreds have died, but before I get involved in this fight, I need to find my parents.

I'm leaving for Mexico with Betty, Tom and Guamán where Bill has offered to help us. From there my plan is to head north to look for you, my grandparents, and Tía Lupita. If you are still in L.A., I hope this datachip will reach you. I'm leaving a copy of my mother's nanotext with Betty and Tom for safekeeping. What I really hope is to find my Mom and Dad and join them in their struggle. After all, I'm not a kid anymore. I'm eighteen now and can help out. Hasta pronto, Tío.

Made in the USA
Coppell, TX
12 August 2023